Haley snuggled under the covers. She was so happy. It was great spending time with her dad in his new place. It was almost as good as having him back home. And at least here she didn't have to listen to any arguing.

Things were going so well—why should she leave?

Haley rolled over. "Tori?" she asked in a whisper. "Are you asleep?"

"Not yet," Tori answered. "What is it?"

"Tori, I've decided to move here with my dad," Haley confided. "You know, for good."

Other Skylark Books you will enjoy
Ask your bookseller for the books you have missed

Anne of Green Gables by L. M. Montgomery

The Great Mom Swap by Betsy Haynes

The Great Dad Disaster by Betsy Haynes

Horse Crazy, The Saddle Club #1
by Bonnie Bryant

Seal Child by Sylvia Peck

The Wild Mustang by Joanna Campbell

Spell It M-U-R-D-E-R by Ivy Ruckman

Pronounce It Dead by Ivy Ruckman

Elvis Is Back, and He's in the Sixth Grade!
by Stephen Mooser

What Is the Teacher's Toupee Doing in the Fish Tank?
by Jerry Piasecki

A NEW
MOVE

Melissa Lowell

Created by Parachute Press

A SKYLARK BOOK
NEW YORK · TORONTO · LONDON · SYDNEY · AUCKLAND

With special thanks to Darlene Parent,
Director of Sky Rink Skating School, New York City

Cover costume by Tania Bass, New York City

RL 5, 009–012

A NEW MOVE

A Skylark Book / March 1996

Skylark Books is a registered trademark of Bantam Books,
a division of Bantam Doubleday Dell Publishing Group, Inc.
Registered in U.S. Patent and Trademark Office and elsewhere.

Silver Blades® is a trademark of Parachute Press, Inc.

Series design: Barbara Berger

All rights reserved.
Copyright © 1996 by Parachute Press
Cover art copyright © 1996 by Frank Morris/Kathryn Manzo
No part of this book may be reproduced or transmitted
in any form or by any means, electronic or mechanical,
including photocopying, recording, or by any information
storage and retrieval system, without permission in
writing from the publisher.
For information address:
Bantam Doubleday Dell Books for Young Readers

If you purchased this book without a cover you should be aware
that this book is stolen property. It was reported as "unsold and
destroyed" to the publisher and neither the author nor the
publisher has received any payment for this "stripped book."

ISBN 0-553-48357-9

Published simultaneously in the United States and Canada

Bantam Books are published by Bantam Books, a division of Bantam
Doubleday Dell Publishing Group, Inc. Its trademark, consisting of
the words "Bantam Books" and the portrayal of a rooster, is
Registered in U.S. Patent and Trademark Office and in other
countries. Marca Registrada. Bantam Books, 1540 Broadway, New
York, New York 10036.

PRINTED IN THE UNITED STATES OF AMERICA

OPM   0 9 8 7 6 5 4 3 2 1

1

Haley Arthur stared at herself in the full-length mirror on the back of her closet door, watching closely as she practiced her new dance moves.

Why can't I get this right? she wondered for about the hundredth time. She sighed and pulled down the oversized black T-shirt she wore over electric-blue leggings. She would just have to try again.

The dance moves were part of her new skating routine. Haley was thirteen and a pairs skater with Silver Blades, one of the country's top skating clubs. She and her partner, Patrick McGuire, were really excited about learning the steps to their new routine.

The moves had been designed especially for Haley and Patrick by Blake Michaels. Blake was a former ice dancer. Now he was a choreographer who created routines to show off the special talents of the skaters in

Silver Blades. Blake said the new steps matched Patrick's energy—and Haley's sense of humor.

Haley pushed her damp auburn bangs off her forehead and sighed in frustration. At the moment, she didn't have much of a sense of humor.

She focused on the mirror again and tried to remember exactly what Blake had shown her. The steps were based on a style called "stomp dancing." Haley had to learn a tricky combination of hand clapping, knee lifts, brackets, tuck behinds, rockers, choctaws, and stomping. The steps would look great once Haley and Patrick performed them in unison. But Haley couldn't manage to master the steps by herself, let alone in time with Patrick.

Not that Patrick was getting it, either, Haley reminded herself. He might be a few years older than Haley, but he'd made as many mistakes as she had at practice that day. In fact, nothing had gone right at practice.

Patrick and I usually have so much fun when we skate, Haley thought. But today it felt like hard work.

Haley flopped down on her bed, shoving her old stuffed animals into a corner by the wall. The rest of her room was a mess, as usual. Clothes and school papers were scattered all over the floor. Her black beanbag chair was so covered with sweaters and skating clothes that Haley could hardly see it.

I should really clean this up, she told herself. But she didn't move. Instead she gazed at the far wall, which was covered with a collage of posters and skating photographs. Usually she felt inspired by looking at pictures of her skating heroes, especially the pairs skaters Jenni Meno and Todd Sand. But not today.

I'll give it one more try, Haley decided. She closed her eyes and pictured herself and Patrick skating side-by-side flying camels. As they came out of the spin, they launched into the series of hand claps and knee slaps while they stomped and turned their skates. Just as Haley began to get a picture of how good it could look, the sound of loud voices coming from downstairs broke her concentration.

"You only think about yourself!" she heard her mother yell.

"Please, Lois, let's not start that again!" her father yelled back.

"It's true," her mother shouted.

"I can't say *anything* around here," her father complained. "All I get are criticisms and accusations!"

Haley pulled a pillow over her head. Her parents were at it again! Lately all they did was yell at each other. It had been going on this way for weeks, ever since her dad had gotten back from his latest business trip.

Not again, she thought. I'll go crazy if I have to listen to them fight all night. If only things would go back to the way they used to be!

When Haley was little, her parents had never yelled at each other. She, her parents, and her younger sister, Morgan, had been a regular, happy family. But not anymore.

Downstairs, the voices grew louder.

"I can't stand this!" Haley groaned. She decided to take a hot shower. The shower would drown out the noise of the argument.

Haley undressed and threw on her robe. She grabbed her waterproof Walkman and dug a favorite tape out from underneath some sweaters. She stormed down the hall to the bathroom. At least I won't have to practice the routine in the shower, she told herself.

She slammed the bathroom door behind her and turned the water on all the way. She slid in her tape and turned the volume way up. She stepped into the shower and let the water pound her shoulders.

She stayed there for a long time. When she was done and had dried off, she turned off the tape and stuck her head out the bathroom door. No more yelling, she noticed with relief.

As she headed down the hall, she stopped in surprise. She heard her mother's voice coming from her sister's bedroom. Morgan was eleven and a half and into horseback riding.

Haley poked her head in the door. Mrs. Arthur was sitting on the bed with Morgan. Their heads were bent over a magazine. Mrs. Arthur seemed perfectly calm now.

"That's a beautiful saddle, Morgan," her mother said. "Wouldn't it be nice to own one like that?"

"It'd be fantastic, Mom," Morgan said happily. "Do you think I really could?"

"It's pretty expensive. We'll have to see," Mrs. Arthur replied.

Watching the two of them, Haley felt a pang of jealousy. She couldn't help feeling left out. Sometimes Mrs. Arthur and Morgan seemed more like sisters than mother and daughter. Haley's mom used to be a rider herself. She was much more interested in Morgan's riding than Haley's skating. Haley wished that her mom would get as excited about her skating equipment as she did about Morgan's riding gear.

Mom *never* looks at skating magazines with me, Haley thought with a scowl. They're so interested in their silly catalog that they don't even see me standing here.

Haley cleared her throat. Mrs. Arthur and Morgan glanced up at her.

"Did you have a good shower, dear?" Haley's mother asked distractedly. She gave Haley a smile and then turned back to the magazine.

As if she really cares about me, Haley thought. "Where's Dad?" she asked.

"Your father went out for a walk," Mrs. Arthur answered. Her voice was cool.

Haley swallowed hard. That meant her father had stormed out of the house. She hated it when he did that. The only thing worse than listening to them argue was the silence after he left.

Why does Mom let him go? Haley wondered. Doesn't she care about him anymore? Why can't she do something to stop him?

"When's he coming back?" Haley demanded.

Her mother was still glancing through the magazine. "In a while," she said.

Haley clenched her hands into fists. "Mom!" she exploded. "I can't believe you! You argue with Dad every single day and then you act like nothing's going on! Everyone in the neighborhood must hear you guys fighting."

"I don't care for your tone of voice, Haley Arthur," her mother responded. "Don't talk to me that way."

"You talk that way to Dad," Haley shot back. "If you really cared, you'd stop fighting with him!"

Morgan suddenly leaped off the bed and began riffling through the stack of magazines on her night table as though she were looking for something. Haley glared at her.

"You're as bad as Mom!" Haley yelled at her sister. "How can you look at stupid horse magazines when our whole family is falling apart?"

"Haley," her mother said sharply, "that's enough. Leave your sister alone."

Morgan narrowed her eyes at her older sister. "You're just like Dad, Haley. Always fighting and yelling at Mom."

Haley gaped. Did Morgan really think the fighting was their father's fault? Leave it to Morgan to be on Mom's side, Haley thought.

"Will both of you please calm down?" Haley's mother cried. "I'm sorry that the situation is hard for you. It's just the way things are right now."

"It's not hard for *me*, Mom," Morgan said in a sugary-sweet voice. She held out a magazine. "I found that other saddle I wanted to show you."

"Just a moment, Morgan." Mrs. Arthur turned to Haley. "Your father and I had a discussion, and we disagreed. It's not the end of the world. People have arguments."

"Why?" Haley said, feeling tears begin to form. "*Why* do you have to fight? Why do you yell at each other all the time?"

Morgan tugged on her mother's sleeve. "Mom, here's the saddle."

Mrs. Arthur sighed. "All right, Haley, since you have to know, your father had a job offer in Canada. I tried to tell him that I'm not moving us that far away. He walked out."

Haley was stunned. Her father was thinking about accepting a job in Canada?

"Mom," Morgan said again, "the saddle."

"Yes, Morgan." Their mother bent over the magazine.

"I'm going to my room," Haley announced. She turned on her heel, marched into her room, and closed the door.

Flopping onto her bed, Haley opened a schoolbook. She had a big history assignment to do. But she couldn't focus on the book in front of her. She kept reading the same page over and over again. Finally she realized she was listening for her father to come home.

As the book slipped from her hands, Haley stared at

the wall. Her dad was so important to her. She was afraid her mother was driving him away. They kept fighting, and he kept storming out of the house.

Haley swallowed. I can't take much more of this, she thought.

What would happen next? she wondered. What if her father *did* take the job in Canada? What if one time he walked out—and he didn't come back?

2

The next morning at the rink, Haley shoved her pur-
ple-and-red parka into her locker and slammed the
door. She was still in a bad mood from the night before.
Her father had come home late, after Haley was in bed.
She had heard her parents talking for a long time in
their bedroom.

Haley changed into practice clothes and sat down to
slip on her skate guards. Just then Tori Carsen and
Nikki Simon came into the locker room.

Tori, a pretty blonde with blue eyes, was a talented
singles skater. She had just won a bronze medal at the
Junior National Figure-Skating Championships. She
was also a good friend of Haley's.

Tori carefully hung her powder-blue parka and
matching gloves in her locker. "Hi, Haley," she said.

"Hi," Nikki added with a little wave. Nikki was a pairs

skater, like Haley. Nikki and her partner, Alex Beekman, had also competed at the Nationals. Nikki had been too nervous to perform well. But Nikki wasn't a quitter. She had been skating extra hard since then.

Nikki put her green jacket away and began brushing her silky brown hair. "It's so cold out today," she remarked. "I can't believe it's almost spring! I can't wait for warm weather."

"Yeah, me too," Haley replied without much enthusiasm.

Tori and Nikki exchanged a puzzled glance as Martina Nemo rushed into the room. Martina was a singles skater. She was good, but not as good as Tori. With her dark hair, olive skin, and big dark eyes, Martina was striking.

"Hi, everyone," she called cheerfully.

"Hey, you guys, wait till you hear Nikki's idea for spring break," Tori said. She pulled a purple velvet skating dress out of her bag. Tori's mother was a clothing designer, and she made all of Tori's skating outfits. Tori was the best-dressed skater Haley knew.

"You know how the World Junior Figure-Skating Championships are going to be on TV?" Nikki asked. "Well, I thought we should all get together and watch."

"That's a great idea," Martina instantly agreed.

Nikki swept her hair into a ponytail. "I bet Alex will be disappointed that he can't come; his family is going to Florida."

"Oh, really?" Tori said. She shot Haley a meaningful glance. Tori knew that Haley had a big crush on Alex.

Haley managed a small smile. Thinking about Alex made her feel better for a moment. A little while ago he'd asked Haley out on a real date. Haley was thrilled. They hadn't actually had the date yet, but Haley was looking forward to it.

Martina sat on the bench to lace her skates. She glanced at Nikki. "Is it really okay with your mom? I mean, isn't she tired, staying up nights with your baby brother and all?"

"She said it's fine," Nikki answered. "Benjamin finally started sleeping through the night. Mom said I can have a whole bunch of kids over for the Worlds. We can make it like a party or something."

"It sounds great," Tori said, her blue eyes sparkling. "But they'll be showing highlights from the Worlds all week. We can't go to your house every day," she told Nikki.

"We could take turns," Martina suggested. "We could start at Nikki's and then watch at different people's houses. Right, Haley?"

"Uh, sure," Haley replied. She wasn't too excited about the idea. She didn't exactly want her friends to be at her house. What if her parents started fighting in front of everyone?

Haley glanced up as Amber Armstrong flew into the locker room. Amber tore off her parka, sweater, and jeans and quickly changed into her practice clothes.

Amber was the newest member of Silver Blades. She was also the youngest in their group of friends—and the most talented. Amber and her mom had come all the way from New Mexico so that Amber could skate with the club.

At first Amber hadn't had any close friends in Silver Blades. But then Haley, Tori, and Nikki had gone to the Nationals in California with Amber. They'd all gotten to know her a little better. And to like her better, too.

Amber gazed around eagerly. "Are you guys talking about the World Juniors?" She threw her skate bag into her locker and slammed the door.

"That's right," Tori answered. She took her skates out of her rose-colored bag and started lacing up.

"I read in *Rinkside* that they're being held in Edmonton, in Alberta, Canada," Amber said. "Didn't they have the Olympics there a few years ago? They must have a really great rink. I'd love to skate there someday."

Haley glanced at Tori. Amber was superambitious, a fact she never bothered to hide. Plus she was Tori's only real skating competition in the club, now that Jill Wong was skating at the International Ice Academy in Denver.

But Tori smiled back at Amber. "Me too," she agreed. "I hear Canada's a great place for skaters."

"Well, I'd better get out and practice, right?" Amber gave a little wave. "See you guys on the ice," she said, hurrying out the door.

Haley stared down at her skates. All the talk about Canada reminded her of her father's job offer. And thinking about that made her remember her parents' big fight. Haley shook her head, as if to erase the memory from her mind.

"Ready," Nikki announced.

"Me too." Martina stood up. "See you guys in a minute." The two girls hurried from the locker room together.

Tori gazed into the mirror and adjusted her skirt. "I *told* my mother I wanted this a little shorter," she complained. Then she turned to Haley and laughed. "All right, Haley, go ahead."

"Huh?" Haley said absentmindedly. "Go ahead and do what?"

"You know, go ahead and let me have it. Tell me that it's the skating that counts, not the dress. Like you always do," Tori said. She rolled her eyes.

"Oh." Haley shrugged. "Yeah, I guess so."

Tori peered at her more closely. "Are you okay? Come to think of it, you haven't teased me once this morning."

Haley swallowed. Everything was definitely not okay, but she didn't know how to explain what she was feeling.

Tori frowned. "Haley, is something wrong?"

Haley hesitated. Tori was a good friend—Haley's best friend in Silver Blades.

"Well, my parents had another fight," Haley admitted. "It was awful. They were yelling and screaming, and then my dad left the house. I wish things would go back to normal. I can't stand this."

"It sure sounds like they've been fighting a lot lately," Tori said. "I guess it must be pretty hard on you and Morgan."

"Oh, Morgan! I don't think she even notices!" Haley cried. "As long as she can go horseback riding, nothing else matters." Haley jabbed at her hair, pushing it out of her eyes.

"I'm afraid everything's going to fall apart," she told Tori. "What if my parents break up? I won't even *have* a family anymore!" Haley felt tears well up in her eyes.

"That's not true," Tori assured her. "I mean, even if your parents do break up, you'll still have a family. Look at me. My parents are divorced, but they're still my parents, right?"

"I guess," Haley replied with her head down.

"It's true," Tori insisted.

"But it's different for you," Haley burst out. "Your parents split up when you were a baby. You barely even *knew* your dad. But I'm used to having both of my parents around. And my dad's the one who cares about me and my skating."

"Your mom cares about you, too," Tori said.

Haley shook her head. "Dad's the one who surprised me in Boston when we were in the *Nutcracker on Ice* show. And he flew out to meet me in California after the Nationals," she said. "Mom never did anything like that."

Tori nodded thoughtfully. "I guess it's the opposite for me," she said slowly. "My mom's the one who's into my skating career."

Haley heard someone clearing her throat. She whirled around. Amber was standing near the lockers.

"Uh, I forgot my warm-up jacket," Amber explained.

Haley felt her face turn red.

"Listen," Amber told her, "I heard what you were saying about your parents. I feel really bad for you."

"Thanks," Haley murmured. She ducked her head in embarrassment.

"You know, my dad had to stay at his job in New Mexico when I came to Seneca Hills," Amber said. "He hasn't been able to visit at all."

"Don't you hate that?" Haley asked.

"Yeah," Amber answered. "Sometimes I wish that I could just *see* him, even for five minutes. And my mom misses him so much. Sometimes she cries when she thinks I'm asleep. And that makes me feel kind of bad." Amber paused. "But they say it's worth it if being here helps with my skating."

"But at least you know that your parents want to be together," Haley pointed out. "I don't even have *that* anymore."

"You don't know that for sure, Haley," Tori said. "Maybe everything will work out okay."

"Maybe," Haley replied. But she doubted it.

The three girls left the locker room together.

Haley slipped off her skate guards and glided to the part of the rink where she and Patrick practiced. Patrick skated up to her. He was wearing faded jeans and a white T-shirt under a funky forest-green vest that really set off his red hair and dark brown eyes. Usually

Haley would have told him that he looked great. But that day she barely nodded to him.

"You're late," Patrick said with a grin. "Hey, for once it's you and not me."

"Sorry," Haley said.

"Sorry?" Patrick continued in a teasing voice. "I can't let you off that easy. I should give you one of those lectures you always give me when *I'm* late."

Haley gave Patrick a halfhearted smile. She wasn't really in the mood for his jokes. Haley noticed their coach, Kathy Bart, standing to one side. Kathy was talking with Amber, whom she also coached.

"I guess we should start without Kathy," Haley said to Patrick.

She loosened up, bending over to stretch her hamstrings. She twisted from side to side and did some deep knee bends. She slowly stretched every muscle. Finally she skated around the rink for a few minutes before gliding back to Patrick.

"Okay, I'm warmed up enough," she said.

"Great. I'm ready. Did you practice the new moves that Blake showed us?" Patrick asked.

"I tried, but I can't get the rhythm right," Haley admitted. "The more I think about it, the more I get confused."

"I know what you mean," Patrick responded. "When Blake does it, it looks so easy. Let's try it together."

"Okay," Haley agreed. But she felt awkward as she and Patrick began their routine.

Maybe it was because Haley had grown so much

taller lately. A growth spurt, Kathy called it. Kathy said that a dramatic change like that could throw both partners off balance.

But whatever the reason, both Haley and Patrick seemed to be having a hard time adjusting.

"Let's start with the side-by-side flying camels and then try the new combination step," Patrick suggested.

Haley nodded. She tried to clear her mind and focus on her skating.

She glided a few feet away from Patrick and took up her start position. She raised her arms and glanced over at Patrick. He nodded, and they began the routine.

It was important for pairs skaters always to keep the same distance apart during side-by-side moves. Some of the jumps and spins were very fast, and a skater could get seriously injured by moving too close. It was one of the things that pairs skaters were judged on at competitions.

From the corner of her eye, Haley watched out for Patrick's shoulders. She performed a series of backward crossovers and then transferred her weight to her left foot. She swung her right leg around in the air, careful to keep her back arched and her chin up. She jumped from her left blade, holding her arms out straight to the side. She wobbled a bit through the spin but kept her balance.

She stepped to the left as she came out of the spin and put her hands together in a loud clap, the first one in the new sequence.

Haley glanced up. Patrick was right next to her! He gaped at her in surprise.

"Haley, what are you doing?" Patrick asked loudly. He skidded to a stop. "When we come out of the camels, we're supposed to go to the right, not the left!" he told her. "You almost crashed into me."

"Are you sure?" Haley asked. She rubbed her face. She felt confused. "I was sure this was the right direction."

"No, that's the *left* direction. The *right* direction is going *right*," Patrick joked. "The last time I checked, I could tell the difference between left and right. How about you?"

"Cut it out," Haley snapped. "You don't have to make a joke out of everything, you know."

"Wow. You sure woke up on the wrong side of the bed today." Patrick stared at her. "You're usually the one making all the jokes. What happened?"

"I'm not in a funny mood, okay?" Haley said, frowning.

"Fine," Patrick replied, making a face. "Be as grouchy as you want."

"What's the matter with you two?" Kathy demanded as she glided over to the pair. "You almost crashed into each other."

"It was a mistake," Haley answered.

"Haley went in the wrong direction," Patrick added. "This new routine Blake gave us is kind of confusing."

"I want both of you to pay more attention," Kathy warned them.

Kathy was a demanding coach—so demanding that her students had nicknamed her "Sarge." Haley knew she'd better shape up, or else she would hear a lot more from Kathy.

Haley did her best. She couldn't quite push her worries about her parents out of her mind, but she skated better.

Kathy seemed satisfied. "Okay, why don't you work on those new steps on your own now?" she suggested. "I'm going to help Amber for a few minutes."

Kathy skated away, and Patrick turned to Haley.

"Okay," he said. "Time to make total fools of ourselves. Let me try it first. See if you have any idea what I'm doing wrong."

Haley sighed. "Okay," she agreed.

She watched Patrick work his way slowly through the new step-and-clap combination.

"I don't know," Haley commented. "It looks kind of funny. I mean, you got a lot of the moves right, but Blake makes it much smoother. It kind of looks like you don't know what you're doing."

"Probably because I don't," Patrick said with a laugh. He shook his head. "You try it and see if you can do any better."

Haley tried the combination. She knew right away that it wasn't coming together. She kept having to stop and think of what she was supposed to do next. It was really frustrating. She got so confused trying to do a double clap under her left knee that she lost her balance and crashed to the ice.

Patrick covered his mouth with one hand, trying not to laugh. "Sorry," he said, giving her a hand to help her up. "You looked so mad, I couldn't help it."

Haley glared at him. Patrick flung an arm around her shoulder. "Hey, I just want you to start laughing again. You seem so down."

Haley had to blink back sudden tears. But she didn't feel like explaining everything to Patrick. She couldn't talk, she was so upset. Still, it was nice to know that he cared.

"Don't worry," Patrick told her. "We'll get it sooner or later."

Haley nodded.

"You'll see," Patrick assured her. "It's just tough learning something brand-new. Besides, you know how hard it is to skate pairs. There's so much to think about. You have to worry about yourself *and* a whole extra person. But we're a great couple."

Haley nodded. She knew how hard it was to be a couple, all right. But the couple she was worried about right now wasn't her and Patrick.

Her mind was on *another* couple—her parents. Would things ever work out between them?

3

Later that day Haley sat in Kathy's office, waiting for her coach to drive her home. Mrs. Arthur's business schedule made it impossible for her to bring Haley to and from practice. She had made a special arrangement with Kathy. And Haley enjoyed spending extra time with her coach off the ice.

She glanced at the familiar things on Kathy's desk. There were her favorite stuffed animals, Porky the Porcupine and a punk-rocker hedgehog. And the dish of butterscotch candies that always sat on the edge of the coach's desk. Haley unwrapped a candy and popped it into her mouth.

The afternoon practice had been difficult for Haley. She hadn't been able to concentrate for more than a few minutes at a time. She'd fallen a lot, too. Patrick had started to get impatient with her. But Haley couldn't help it. She just couldn't keep her mind on the new steps. She kept thinking about her family. It had definitely been one of her worst skating days ever.

Haley examined a framed photograph that stood on the desk. It had been taken several years ago, before Kathy became a coach. The photo showed Kathy with her family at the Nationals. Kathy had placed fourth. Her mom and dad were standing on either side of her, beaming happily. Haley felt a stab of envy. Kathy's parents seemed so proud of their daughter.

Haley quickly replaced the photo when she heard the door open behind her.

"Sorry to keep you waiting, Haley," Kathy said in a cheerful voice. "But I'm almost finished. Come with me while I drop these flyers off around the rink. They're about a change in the practice schedule. All set?"

"Ready," Haley answered, grabbing her skate bag and parka.

She followed Kathy down the hall between the two rinks of the arena—the figure-skating rink and the rink used for ice hockey. Kathy stopped to drop off the flyers at the first-aid center, the Silver Blades costume department, the snack bar, and the weight and exercise training rooms. They passed the pro shop, and the owner, Toby Mullen, waved as they went by.

"Good night!" Kathy called.

Toby smiled at Haley. Haley gave him back a small smile. She and Kathy continued through the lobby and finally pushed through the double swinging doors to the rink. Outside, the early-evening air was brisk. Haley gazed at the last traces of sunset while she waited for Kathy to unlock the doors of her tan Buick. Haley slid into the car with a sigh.

Kathy glanced at her with concern.

"You seem a little down, Haley," Kathy commented as she started the car. "And I noticed you took a lot of falls today. Are you okay?"

"I'm a little sore," Haley answered with a shrug.

"I like to take a long, hot bath after a rough day. Maybe that's what you should do tonight," Kathy suggested.

She pulled out of the parking lot and headed toward Main Street. "It's a good way to relax," Kathy added. "And to get things off your mind."

"I guess," Haley replied. She wondered what things would be like at home that night. Would her parents be fighting again? A hot bath couldn't get that kind of trouble off her mind.

They drove in silence. Haley glanced out the car window at the shops on Main Street. She usually liked to check out the windows of the secondhand boutique, Retro Rosie's, and the sporting-goods store, All-Athlete's Gear. But that evening she wasn't even interested. She was thinking about how much she dreaded going home.

Kathy gave her a sympathetic look. "I know how frustrated you must be. It's tough to hit a block in your routine," the coach remarked. "Especially when you're working with a partner."

Haley bit her lip. She wished she could tell Kathy

what was *really* bothering her. But she couldn't. It was just too embarrassing. Haley thought about the photograph on Kathy's desk. Kathy's family was happy. Haley couldn't imagine Kathy's parents ever screaming at each other the way hers did.

"You and Patrick will work this out," Kathy assured her. "Give it time."

"Thanks, Kathy," Haley replied.

The coach soon pulled into the Arthurs' driveway. "See you in the morning, Haley," she said.

"Okay," Haley responded. "Thanks for the ride."

Haley trudged toward the front door. She stepped onto the plush rug in the entryway and listened. Everything was quiet. She hung her parka in the hall closet and carried her bags upstairs to her room. Then she headed to the kitchen for a snack.

In the hallway Haley noticed a light coming from under Morgan's door. She had an idea. Maybe if she and Morgan got together and asked their parents to stop fighting so much, things would get better.

Haley stuck her head into Morgan's bedroom. "Morgan?"

"Oh, hi, Haley." Morgan was standing in front of her bulletin board. Next to her was a chair piled with ribbons that she had won for horseback riding. Morgan had separated the ribbons by color. She tilted her head to one side.

"What do you think?" Morgan asked. "Should I hang all the same-color ribbons together, or make a pattern?"

"How about all the same together?" Haley replied in a friendly voice.

Morgan nodded and began to arrange the ribbons again.

"Um, Morgan?" Haley began. "Can I ask you a question? You know, about Mom and Dad?"

Morgan frowned. She didn't look up from the ribbons. "Sure," she replied with a shrug.

Then stop playing with those dumb ribbons! Haley thought, feeling annoyed. "If you'd look at me, it'd be easier to talk to you," she said.

"You can talk to me," Morgan said. She fussed with a ribbon on the bulletin board.

Haley tried to ignore the sinking feeling in her stomach. "Morgan, this is important," she said in her most serious tone of voice.

"So are my ribbons," Morgan snapped.

Haley gave up. "Do you know where Mom and Dad are?" she asked.

"No, I don't. Is that your big, important question?" Morgan whirled around. She shook her head impatiently. "They're not here, okay? You act like it's the end of the world or something."

"Well, excuse me," Haley retorted. "And no, that wasn't the question. If you'd stop thinking about your dumb ribbons for a few minutes, I'd tell you what I really want. It's about Mom and Dad and the way they've been fighting."

Morgan gazed at Haley with tears in her eyes. "Why can't you just leave them alone, Haley?"

Haley stared at her, dumbfounded. "We *can't* leave them alone. Don't you see?" Haley cried. "They're fighting all the time. Someone has to make them stop. I thought if you and I went to them together and told them that—"

"I don't *want* to go to them!" Morgan interrupted. "I don't want to tell them anything! All this talking just makes everyone fight more." She choked back a sob. "Why do you have to get into everything, Haley? Maybe it's none of your business!"

Haley gaped at her sister in disbelief. "Not my business?"

"I just want everybody to leave me alone!" Morgan wailed. She glanced at the ribbons in her hands. "Now you made me lose track of what I was doing."

"Fine!" Haley exclaimed. "Go back to your stupid ribbons. Just do nothing. See if I care!" She slammed the door and stomped down the hall to her own room.

Her stomach rumbled. She had completely forgotten about a snack. Haley opened her schoolbag and dumped her books out onto her bed. She was supposed to read a whole chapter in history that night. And she had to finish an entire sheet of geometry problems.

She stared at her books without moving. She knew she should start her homework. But she couldn't. She felt as if her whole life was falling apart. And compared to that, schoolwork seemed about the least important thing in the world.

4

Half an hour later, Haley heard the front door slam. She ran down the spiral staircase two steps at a time. She found both her parents in the kitchen. Her mother and father stood next to each other, unpacking a bag of Chinese food.

"Where were you guys?" Haley asked them.

"Oh, your mom and I met downtown," her father answered.

He and her mother exchanged glances.

"We needed to discuss a few things," Mrs. Arthur added. "And we decided to pick up some Chinese food. We got your favorites—shrimp with broccoli, and egg rolls."

"Mmm, that smells great!" Haley said. She loved Chinese food.

"I hope you're hungry, Hals," Mrs. Arthur said. She

set another two cartons on the counter. "Could you get out the plates and silverware?" she asked her husband.

Haley smiled. Her parents were getting along better than they had in weeks. Maybe they had made up for good.

"Why don't you tell your sister it's time for dinner?" her father suggested. "And afterward we have something we want to talk to you girls about."

"Okay," Haley agreed.

As she ran upstairs to get Morgan, Haley wondered what her parents wanted to talk to them about.

They seem a lot more relaxed than they have been, she noted to herself. Maybe they want to apologize to us for all the fighting. Maybe they want to tell us that they're going to try to get along from now on.

Then Morgan will see that I was right, Haley thought. She stuck her head into her sister's room.

"Hey, Morgan," she announced. "It's dinnertime. They got Chinese!"

"Really?" Morgan perked up.

"Yeah. And they want to talk to us about something important after dinner. Come on!" Haley exclaimed.

Dinner was delicious. Haley felt good for the first time in weeks. She was so happy to see her family together.

"I know I'm going to regret it, but I have to eat the last egg roll," her father said. "Unless you want it, Haley?"

"No, Dad, go ahead, I'm stuffed," Haley said, pushing away her plate.

"Well, you'll probably have to *roll* me up the stairs," her dad said with a twinkle in his eye. He squirted some sauce on his plate and started dipping his egg roll in it.

"Very funny, Dad," Haley said with a grin.

Morgan groaned. "Dad, you always tell the corniest jokes. I guess that's where Haley gets it from."

Haley shot her sister a warning look. But she didn't say anything. She didn't want to spoil the mood by getting mad at Morgan.

"Yeah, Haley's a chip off the old block," her father replied. "Bad jokes are a fine Arthur tradition. Right, Lois?" he added, looking at his wife.

"At least for one branch of the family," Mrs. Arthur answered.

"Not *my* branch," Morgan insisted.

"Wait and see, Morgan. It might catch up with you later." Mr. Arthur chuckled. He finished the last bite of his egg roll.

Haley stood up to clear the dishes. She reached for her father's plate. "Done, Dad?" she asked.

"That's okay, Hals, just leave it," her mother said. She dabbed her lips with her napkin. "I'll clean up later."

Haley glanced at her mother in surprise. First Chinese food, and now no chores? She and Morgan *always* had to clean up after dinner. What's going on here? she wondered.

"Let's go into the living room," her mother suggested. "We'll be more comfortable in there."

Haley felt her stomach do a flip-flop as she followed her parents into the living room. Mr. and Mrs. Arthur sat on the couch. Haley flung herself into the over-stuffed armchair next to them. Morgan sat cross-legged on the floor near her mother. The two girls gazed at their parents expectantly. Haley licked her lips. Her mouth was a little dry.

Everyone was silent for a moment.

"You girls know that we love you very much," Mrs. Arthur began.

Haley and Morgan exchanged a nervous glance.

"And we want what is best for you," her mother went on. "What's best for the family."

Haley nodded, but she felt numb. She noticed lines forming on her mother's forehead. Why does she look so worried if she's talking about what's best for us? Haley wondered. We all know what's best for us—to stay together and be a happy family again.

I'm starting to get a bad feeling about this, Haley thought. She shifted her legs to the other side of the chair.

"What your mother is trying to say," her father put in, "is that we know our arguing has been very hard on you girls."

Haley glanced over at Morgan. Her sister was staring down at her feet.

"Your mother and I have given this a lot of thought," her father continued. "And we have an idea. A way to make things better for everyone." He paused. "We decided that the two of us should spend some time away from each other."

Haley felt as though her heart had stopped. Did he say that they were going to spend time *apart*?

How much time? she wondered anxiously. What did this mean? She felt sick. She couldn't even say anything. Instead she swallowed hard and waited for her father to continue.

"Your mother and I are separating," he finished. "We won't be living together anymore."

Haley found herself staring at her feet dangling off the side of the armchair. Her eyes filled with tears, and everything went out of focus. She blinked.

There it was. The thing that she was most afraid of. It was actually happening. Her parents were splitting up.

She couldn't believe it.

"But what about us?" Morgan asked. "What's going to happen to us?" She began to cry.

"Come here, Morgan," her mother said gently. She held out her arms.

Morgan crawled into her mother's lap and cried on her shoulder. Haley stared at them, feeling more alone than ever. She gazed at her father, but he was staring down at his shoes. Haley was in shock. She wanted to ask her parents to change their minds, but she couldn't get the words out.

"Your father and I haven't been getting along for a long time now," Haley's mother continued. "We still love each other. And of course we love the two of you. But we need time to work things out."

"What about us?" Haley managed to ask.

Mrs. Arthur took a deep breath. "You girls will stay with me. Everything will be like it always is, except that your father won't be living here. We'll still be a family," she assured them. "We just won't be a family that's together all the time."

Haley felt as though she could hardly breathe. Her father was really leaving. What would she do without him? She didn't want to be stuck alone with her mother and Morgan.

She glanced at her sister crying in her mother's arms. There's no place for me here, Haley thought. This is the worst thing that could happen to me!

"Oh, Mom," Morgan wailed. Their mother squeezed Morgan tighter.

Haley sat bolt upright in her chair. "Wait a minute," she said. "What if I don't *want* to stay here? What if I want to live with Dad?" She glanced at her father. "Dad, can I go with you? Please?"

Haley's father reached out and took her hand. "Haley, I'm sorry," he answered, squeezing her hand. "You can't live with me. It just wouldn't work out."

"Why not?" Haley demanded.

"Your father accepted the job in Canada, Haley," her mother explained. "He's moving to a town called Edmonton. You'll have to stay here in Seneca Hills. That way you and Morgan will be able to continue with school and your skating and riding."

"But that's not what I want!" Haley exploded. She

glared at both her parents angrily. "This is so unfair! How can it be all decided, just like that?"

"It's for the best, Haley," her father insisted. "Your mother and I feel comfortable with this decision. We're sure that in time you girls will, too."

"I'll *never* like it!" Haley screamed. "I'll always hate this!" Her tears were flowing now, and the words came tumbling out.

"You never ask what I want," she screamed at her mother. Haley leaped to her feet. "You never ask how I feel about anything! All you care about is yourself and Morgan's stupid horses!"

"Haley, please don't act this way," her father said.

"Why? No one cares about me," she cried. "Well, fine! I don't need any of you!"

She raced to her room and slammed the door. She threw herself onto the bed, sobbing. She had never felt so alone in her life. Her father was leaving, and her mother didn't care how she felt!

I wish they'd start fighting again, she thought. It would be better than this. Anything would be better than this!

Haley wept until she was too tired to cry anymore. She rolled onto her back and gazed out the window. A single star shone in the sky. Haley stared at it.

Please, she thought, make this all a bad dream. When I wake up in the morning, let everything be the way it was before.

5

"Hi, Haley," Tori called cheerfully as she breezed into the weight-training room at the rink.

Tori wore a hot-pink unitard. Her blond waves were tied back in a ponytail. She plunked herself down at the leg-press machine next to Haley. They were alone in the room. Haley paused in her workout on the sit-up board.

"Hi, Tori," Haley said. She rubbed her eyes. She knew they were still puffy from all her crying the night before.

"Hey, what's wrong? Were you crying?" Tori asked. She let down the weights in the leg press.

"Yeah." Haley felt fresh tears form in her eyes. "My parents are splitting up," she blurted out.

"Oh, no!" Tori exclaimed. "Are you sure? When did you find out? What happened?"

"They told us last night after dinner," Haley explained, blinking back the tears. "They said they weren't getting along, and they decided my dad should move out. The worst part is, my dad's moving all the way to Canada!"

"That's so far away!" Tori exclaimed.

"I know," Haley replied with a deep sigh. "I asked if I could live with him instead. But he said I can't because he's moving. His company is sending him there."

"I feel so bad for you." Tori wrinkled her forehead. "Can I help? I mean, all your friends are here, and—"

"Oh, Tori, please don't tell anybody yet," Haley pleaded. "I don't want them feeling sorry for me and stuff. I don't think I could take it."

"I won't say a word. I promise. Not even to my mother," Tori vowed.

~ ~

"Who can tell me why George Washington crossed the Delaware?" Mrs. Belding asked.

Haley stared into space while the teacher droned on. It was later that afternoon, and Haley was in history class. She couldn't pay attention. Instead she took out a pen and doodled in the margin of her textbook.

She drew angry faces in the chapter she was supposed to have read. She hadn't done any of her homework the night before.

Mrs. Belding talked on and on. Haley flipped to another page and yawned. Then, suddenly, she realized that the teacher was staring right at her.

"Haley?" Mrs. Belding said. "Could you please answer me?"

Haley's stomach plunged. "Uh, what was the question?" she asked.

"Haley, where have you been?" Mrs. Belding replied. "Certainly not in class with the rest of us. I asked you to describe the conditions that winter at Valley Forge."

"Um, it was very cold that winter at Valley Forge?" Haley tried. There was laughter from the class.

"I'm sure we all know *that*, Haley." Mrs. Belding frowned.

Haley glanced at the clock. The bell should ring any second, she noticed.

"Could you tell us something a little more specific?" Mrs. Belding went on. "Something from the chapter you were supposed to read?"

Before Haley could answer, the bell rang. "Sorry, Mrs. Belding." Haley scrambled out of her chair. "I have to go to math class now."

Haley grabbed her books and ran out the door without looking at Mrs. Belding.

Whew, that was close, she thought. I bet Mrs. Belding is really mad at me now.

She hurried to her math class. She didn't have her geometry homework, either. Ms. Cantore's not going to be happy with me, Haley realized. Maybe I should cut class and say that I wasn't feeling well.

Haley hesitated outside the door to the geometry

classroom. Before she could decide what to do, she felt a hand on her shoulder. It was Ms. Cantore, dressed in her usual jacket and skirt and clunky black heels.

"Uh, hi, Ms. Cantore," Haley said. I can't cut class now that she's seen me, she thought.

"Hello, Haley," Ms. Cantore replied. "Ready for geometry?"

Haley faked a smile. She walked into the classroom with her teacher.

"All right, students," Ms. Cantore said briskly. "Let's go over the problems you were assigned and correct them in class."

Ms. Cantore turned to the blackboard and began writing out the solution to the first problem. Haley couldn't believe it. What a lucky break! she told herself. I can just copy down the answers and hand them in! Haley started scribbling furiously.

Her head was bent over her paper when she noticed a sudden quiet in the room. She gazed up to find Ms. Cantore standing right in front of her. The teacher reached for Haley's paper and examined it.

"I thought so! You haven't done the problems at all. Haley, you know you're not supposed to just copy the answers," the teacher scolded. "Why didn't you do the assignment?"

Haley hung her head in silence.

"I'm waiting," Ms. Cantore said.

Why? Haley thought miserably. Why? Because my dad's moving to Canada and my whole life is falling apart. Math doesn't seem too important right now! That's why!

But there was no way Haley was going to say that in front of the whole class.

"I, uh—I don't have a reason," Haley replied.

"Well, then, let's see what your parents have to say about that," her teacher responded.

Haley almost laughed out loud. Sure, see if *they* care, she thought. My parents are too busy with their own problems to notice mine. If they cared, they wouldn't be splitting up, she thought with a smirk.

Ms. Cantore frowned. "Did I say something funny? Let's see how amused you are in detention." The teacher slapped Haley's paper back onto her desk and returned to the blackboard.

Haley slumped down in her chair and stared out the window. Detention! She couldn't believe it. She'd never gotten detention before.

She blinked back tears. Ms. Cantore didn't understand. Haley couldn't stay late after school. She needed to get to skating practice. But she couldn't say that to Ms. Cantore—not while her teacher was so mad.

Haley slumped in her seat. It was all so unfair! Everything was going wrong. And it was all her parents' fault!

6

Haley was having trouble at afternoon practice. She took a deep breath and tried to focus. Blake Michaels, the choreographer, was repeating something to her and Patrick.

"You've got to do these steps over and over again," Blake said.

Haley gazed at the handsome, dark-haired choreographer without really seeing him.

"You have to know the routine so well that you don't have to think about it. Then you'll relax, feel the rhythm, and enjoy it. Right?" Blake raised his eyebrows.

Haley nodded, but she wasn't really listening. Her stomach felt too fluttery for her to pay attention.

She had cut detention. She had to. No way was she

going to miss practice. She and Patrick really needed to work on this routine.

Besides, Haley thought, it's been a really bad day. I *deserve* my skating time. I'll make it up somehow, she promised herself.

"Okay," Blake said, "why don't you both try it on your own? Work at your own pace until you're ready to put the whole sequence together."

"Okay, Blake," Patrick replied. "Thanks." He turned to Haley. "I bet we can do it," he said with enthusiasm. "Let's start with the side-by-side camels."

Haley ran her fingers through her hair. She shook out her arms and legs and tried to clear her mind.

She and Patrick sailed through the camel spins. Then they began the combination steps. Haley did a few of the hand claps and foot stomps right. But she ended up confused again.

She sighed in frustration and glanced over at Patrick. He looked awkward, but he was doing the steps faster than before.

"You're getting better," Haley called to him. I wish I could say the same thing about myself, she thought.

Haley tried once more. But after a few stomps, brackets, claps, and knee lifts, she was even more confused. And she knew it looked terrible.

Patrick glided up to her. "Why don't we try watching each other's hands and feet?" he suggested.

"Okay," Haley replied. "You start."

Patrick faced Haley so that they were toe to toe. He started with two brackets and three hand claps, and then did a knee lift. Then he clapped his hands twice below his lifted knee. He straightened his legs, stomping twice.

"Your turn," he said.

Haley bit her lip. She repeated Patrick's moves exactly.

"That's right!" Patrick cried.

"So far, so good," Haley said with relief.

"This is like when we learned the star-lift," Patrick reminded her. "Remember? We thought we'd never get it. But we did."

"Right," Haley replied, trying to sound enthusiastic. Patrick was really trying, and she didn't want to let him down.

Patrick started on the next section of the combination. This time he clapped four times, stomped twice, and did a double choctaw. Then he clapped twice before beginning backward crossovers and launching into a sit spin. He completed the spin, rose to his full height, and stomped again. Haley repeated the pattern exactly.

"I've got it!" she cried, feeling better than she had all day. "It's kind of like tap dancing," she remarked.

"Yeah, or like flamenco dancing," Patrick added. "I saw that kind of Spanish dancing once. It was at a restaurant in Spain. I went there with my folks one summer on vacation. We had a great time."

"I bet," Haley said. Suddenly she didn't feel so happy. She wished Patrick hadn't mentioned his parents—or their family vacation. She'd probably never take a family vacation again.

She remembered the vacations her family had taken when she and Morgan were little. Only the summer before, they had all gone to Florida. Haley had spent every day splashing in the surf with her dad.

She felt tears spring to her eyes. She blinked furiously so that Patrick wouldn't see.

But Patrick was busy with the next section of their routine. He did a single clap, two three-turns in a row with legs crossed over, a knee lift, and a clap under his knee, followed by a quick pair of stomps, all to the right. Then he repeated everything to the left. Then he repeated all the moves again, but twice as fast. Haley was totally lost.

She tried the routine but made a mess of it. Patrick sighed, but he didn't say anything.

Haley's cheeks flamed in embarrassment. "Wait," she said. "I know I can get this."

"Well, it's practically time to go home," Patrick said cheerfully. "Maybe you'll do better tomorrow."

"Just a second!" Haley insisted. "I said I could do it!" She tried the routine again. But she stomped when she was supposed to clap.

"It's okay," Patrick said. "Let's cut practice short today. I mean, there's no point getting all worked up about it, right?"

"I'm *not* worked up about it!" Haley exclaimed.

"Relax." Patrick smiled. "You need a little more time, okay?" He patted her on the shoulder.

Haley angrily shrugged off his hand. "Don't talk to

me that way!" she shouted. "You're not so great! You don't know all of it, either."

"I know more than you," Patrick shot back. "What's your problem, anyway? These steps aren't *that* hard."

"Maybe *you're* the problem," Haley shouted. "Maybe I need a new partner!"

Patrick's cheeks flushed red. "Well, maybe you do!" he cried. He whirled on his skates and sped to the barrier.

Haley glared after him. Practice was obviously over. She waited until Patrick disappeared into the boys' locker room. Then she skated to the boards and leaned against the barrier.

She felt miserable inside. Everything was going so badly. Her parents were splitting up, she'd been fighting with her sister, she was in trouble at school and worried about cutting detention—and now her skating was terrible, too.

She glided off the ice and pulled on her skate guards. As she started toward the locker room, she heard someone call her name. She glanced toward the front doors.

"Dad!" she cried in surprise. Her father was walking through the big swinging doors!

Haley hurried over to him and wrapped him in a big hug. "Hi, Dad," she said. "What're you doing here? Is everything okay?"

"I just wanted to surprise you," Mr. Arthur replied. "I thought maybe you and I could go out to dinner."

"Just us?" Haley asked.

"Just you and me, kid," her father said with a wink. "That is, if you want to."

"Want to? Of course I want to!" Haley cried. "I have to change. But I'll be back in a minute."

Haley raced into the locker room and sat down on a bench to unlace her skates. Nikki was also changing.

"You sure look happy," Nikki commented.

Haley grinned at her. "Yeah, I guess so. My dad's taking me out to eat."

"Sounds like fun," Nikki said.

"Um, yeah." Haley hadn't told Nikki that her parents were splitting up. But maybe that night she could convince her dad not to go through with it. Then she wouldn't have to tell anyone anything!

Haley pulled on her jeans and sweater and tossed her things into her skate bag. She grabbed her schoolbag, too. "See you tomorrow, Nikki."

Haley hurried back to where her father was waiting. It was just like him to surprise her with something special. She smiled happily. Dinner was going to be great!

7

"**D**id Mom call Kathy?" Haley asked as she and her father walked through the lobby of the rink. "To let her know that you're taking me home," she added.

Mr. Arthur stopped in his tracks. "Oh, right, your mother. I meant to call her. But I didn't get to it," he admitted.

"You mean you didn't tell Kathy or Mom?" Haley was surprised.

"I was so busy at work that I forgot." Her father fished in his pockets. "Here's a quarter. Call your mom and tell her we're going out for dinner."

Haley dropped her bags and headed to the pay phone. She dialed her mother's number at the office.

"Lois Arthur Interiors," her mother answered.

"Hi, Mom," Haley said. "It's me."

"Hi, Hals. Is everything okay?" Mrs. Arthur asked.

"Everything's fine," Haley assured her. "I just wanted to let you know that Dad's here. He wants to take me out to dinner tonight. Okay? I'll tell Kathy that he'll drive me home."

"He didn't mention anything to me about it," her mother said. "But I guess it's okay. It'll be nice for you to spend some time together."

"Thanks, Mom," Haley said.

"I'd like to spend time with you, too," her mother added.

"You would?" Haley asked. "Us alone, or you, me, and Morgan?"

"Well, either way," her mother answered. She was silent a moment. "It made me very unhappy to see you so upset last night," she finally said.

"Oh, well . . ." Haley paused. If her mother was so upset, why didn't she want to spend time alone with Haley? Her dad did.

Her mother didn't say anything more. "Well, bye, Mom," Haley told her. "I'll see you later."

"Okay. Bye, Haley," her mother answered.

Haley hung up and hurried to Kathy's office. She poked her head in the door.

"Kathy," she announced, "I'm going out to dinner with my dad. So you won't need to drive me home today."

"That sounds nice," Kathy answered, glancing up from some paperwork. "I have a lot to do here tonight anyway. Have fun!" She gave a wave.

Haley ran back to the lobby and picked up her bags.

"Everything's set," she told her father happily. "Let's go! I'm starved."

A little while later, Haley and her father were sitting at a front table at Giovanni's, an Italian restaurant not far from the Seneca Hills Ice Arena. The table was set with a pretty red cloth, white napkins, fresh flowers, and a candle in a glass. Haley studied the menu, but she already knew what she wanted. Lasagna was her favorite Italian dish.

The waiter came by with some breadsticks. "Are you ready to order?" he asked.

"Lasagna," Haley and her father said at the same time. They laughed.

"You and I are so alike, Haley," her father said. "I'm really going to miss spending time with you. That's why I wanted to spend some time together tonight. I leave for Edmonton on Saturday."

Haley's heart sank. So much for persuading him not to go.

"I didn't realize you were leaving so soon," Haley said.

"Actually, I moved my things into a hotel this morning," Mr. Arthur told her.

"Oh." Haley felt crushed. "Why?" Suddenly she felt a huge lump in her throat.

"It seemed like the best idea. I wanted to give you guys a chance to get used to my being gone."

"Do you really have to go, Dad?" Haley was trying hard not to cry.

"Yeah, I do," Mr. Arthur said gently. "I wish things could be different, but life doesn't always turn out the way we'd like. Still, there are a few things that will never change."

"Like what?" Haley asked, looking up at her father hopefully.

"I'm always going to love you and your sister. And I want you to know how proud your mother and I are of both of you," her father said.

"Mom's only proud of Morgan," Haley said. "She doesn't really care about me. Or my skating."

Her father frowned. "Of course she does, Haley." He paused. "You know I'm your number-one skating fan. But we both love you very much," he insisted.

"I guess," Haley said with a sigh. "But I've always felt like you and I are a team, the way that Mom and Morgan are a team. With you gone, it's going to feel like I'm on my own."

"Haley, try not to be so hard on your mother. You won't be alone, and you know it," her father chided her.

Haley stared at the napkin in her lap. He doesn't understand, she thought. He doesn't realize what it's like when he's not around.

"Your mom and Morgan are horse nuts," he said. He grinned and gave a whinny. He often did that to tease Morgan and his wife when they talked about horses too much.

Haley had to laugh.

"I like it when you smile," her father said. "Keep smiling. And remember—you can count on *both* of us. Your mom and me. Always." Haley's father reached across the table and squeezed her hand.

The waiter arrived with their dinners. Her dad dug in. To Haley's surprise, she was hungry, too. She and her dad didn't say much while they ate. But Haley didn't mind. She loved that they could be happy together without saying a word.

"That was delicious," Mr. Arthur said after they finished the meal. He pushed his plate away. "But there's no room for dessert," he pretended to complain. "How about you?" he asked Haley.

"I'm full, too," she agreed.

"But we'll have ice cream anyway. Right?" he teased.

"Right!" Haley replied, as she always did.

Haley and her father grinned at each other. Mom never jokes with me this way! Haley thought. I'm really going to miss Dad. Her eyes filled up with tears.

Mr. Arthur ordered the ice cream. "Try to cheer up," he said as they ate. "I mean, being apart from you will be hard on me, too," he told her. "Talking with you at the end of the day, and hearing about school and the rink—that's one of the things I always look forward to. But that doesn't have to stop. You can call me, and write. And sometimes you can come visit me in Edmonton."

"Okay." Haley managed a smile.

"That's better!" Her father glanced at his watch. "Wow. It's getting late. I'd better take you home."

Haley didn't say much in the car. Finally Mr. Arthur pulled into the driveway. Haley leaned over to give him a kiss good night.

"This is really weird," she said. "Can't you even come in with me?"

"I'd rather not," he replied.

Haley nodded, trying to look cheerful.

"Well, sweet dreams, Haley. I'll see you soon," he said. He gave her a big hug good-bye.

Haley climbed out of the car. She opened the front door and turned to wave good-bye. Tears tickled the back of her throat. She swallowed and walked into the house. It was just her mother, Morgan, and her now.

From now on, Haley thought, nothing will ever be the same.

8

Haley woke up late Sunday morning and lay in bed thinking. She had always loved Sundays. When her dad wasn't traveling on business, they always went to the store together. They would buy the paper and on the way back they'd stop for donuts. On nice afternoons they would go for a walk or play Frisbee in the park. But no more. Her dad had left for Canada the day before. And things were already different.

Haley sighed and pulled herself out of bed. Sunday was the one day she didn't have skating practice. Usually she didn't even think about skating. But that day Patrick was on her mind. Their Saturday practice had been awkward. Haley hadn't known what to say to him about their fight, so she'd said nothing. Patrick hadn't mentioned it, but he was tense and silent. Still, Haley wasn't about to back down. Patrick had no right to be so critical.

Haley changed out of her pajamas into black leggings and a huge white turtleneck with green polka dots. She glanced at her desk and groaned. She couldn't face her schoolwork. It was too hard to concentrate on assignments when she felt so sad.

I have so much homework now, I could work all day and still not get it done, she thought. What am I going to do? I'll really be in trouble tomorrow.

She decided to have breakfast. I'll feel better once I have food in my stomach, she told herself.

She went into the bathroom and tugged a comb through her hair and brushed her teeth. Then she ran down the spiral stairs. The kitchen was quiet and empty.

Haley poured cornflakes into a bowl. As she reached for the milk carton, she glanced into the living room. Morgan sat in front of the TV. Haley carried her breakfast into the living room.

"What's on, Morgan?" Haley asked as she plopped down in her favorite armchair.

"It's the video Mom took last month. At the trials for the Junior League Horse Show," Morgan answered. She didn't take her eyes off the screen.

"Boy, you're like a zombie when you watch your horse videos," Haley grumbled.

Morgan ignored her. Haley couldn't understand her sister. She hadn't said a word about their father moving out. She just kept doing the same things that she always did. Haley thought she was even *more* into her horses than usual. If that was possible.

Haley tried watching the video for a few minutes, but she couldn't get interested in it.

"What's the big deal?" Haley asked out loud. "It's the same thing over and over again. The riders all jump the same fence. You can barely tell them apart."

"Just like skating," Morgan muttered.

Haley shrugged. She finished her cereal and drank the last of the milk in her bowl. Mrs. Arthur entered the living room.

"Haley! You're not supposed to eat in here," her mother scolded. "That's why we have a breakfast nook in the kitchen."

"But you don't have a TV in the kitchen," Haley replied. She didn't look at her mother as she swung her legs over the side of the armchair and got up.

"Because it's nicer to talk to each other than to watch TV when we eat," Mrs. Arthur retorted. "It's more of a family feeling."

Haley stalked into the kitchen to rinse out her bowl. Family feeling, that's a good one, she thought with a smirk. We don't even *have* a real family anymore. Haley shoved her bowl into the dishwasher and let the door slam shut.

She sighed. She wished she were with her father right then. Well, why not? she wondered. He said I could visit him in Canada.

How soon could she go? How long could she stay? Suddenly she froze. Why not stay for good? Why not move to Canada? It would mean leaving all her friends in Seneca Hills. And leaving Silver Blades. But it might be worth it if she could be with her dad.

Haley raced back out into the living room. Mrs. Arthur was watching the riding video with Morgan. Haley perched on the couch, waiting for the right moment to speak. Suddenly Morgan's picture flickered on the TV. Her mother leaned forward to watch the tape of Haley's sister jumping the same old fence.

"Morgan, that's your best jump ever!" Mrs. Arthur clapped her hands. Haley squinted at the screen. She supposed her mother knew what she was talking about, but she hadn't noticed anything different. "Your point of balance in the saddle is exactly right," Mrs. Arthur went on. "That's the seat you should have all the time."

"Mom?" Haley said. "Can I ask you something?"

"Sure, Hals," her mother responded. But Mrs. Arthur didn't take her eyes off the tape.

Haley scowled. Why is it that whenever something's important to *me*, Mom is too involved with Morgan's riding to pay attention? she wondered. Dad should see us like this, she thought. Then he'd know what it's really like when he's not around.

The tape ended, and Morgan leaped up to rewind it.

"Listen, Mom," Haley began. "Dad said I could visit him sometime. And I want to go as soon as possible."

Mrs. Arthur didn't answer. She stared at the blank TV screen.

"Mom?" Haley repeated.

"Yes, Haley, I heard you," Mrs. Arthur replied. "I'm thinking. I'm not sure how I feel about it."

"It's not up to you," Haley retorted. "It's up to Dad and me. And we both think it's a great idea."

"Haley, please," her mother said impatiently. "You don't understand the whole situation. Edmonton is far away. And your father would be at work most of the time. I'm not sure it's the best idea right now."

Haley felt her cheeks grow hot. "That's not fair!" she exclaimed. "Dad wants me to go, and I'm going!"

Morgan used the remote control to turn up the volume on the video.

"Stop it, Haley," Mrs. Arthur replied, raising her voice. "*I* make the decisions around here. I didn't say you couldn't *ever* go. I said it's not a good idea to go right now."

"Well, I don't agree," Haley shouted, leaping off the couch. "You don't care what I think!" She was really yelling now, and she couldn't seem to stop herself. "You don't want me to see Dad because you're jealous. You're jealous because we get along so well!"

"Haley, that's not true!" her mother cried. "I think it's *wonderful* that you and your father are close. But I'm still your mother. And I still decide what's best for you."

"All you care about is Morgan and her horses," Haley shrieked.

"Haley, stop it this instant! I will not have you talk to me like that!" her mother said furiously.

Haley glared at her mother and at her sister, who didn't glance away from the television set.

"If it weren't for you, Dad would still be here," Haley shouted. "This is all your fault! Dad's gone because of you, and you don't even care. You don't know what it means to me!" Haley began sobbing. "No one cares about what I think or what I want! It's *my* life, too, you know! I hate being here with you! I hate this house!"

Haley ran from the room. She grabbed her parka from the hall closet, yanked the front door open, and slammed it behind her.

Haley raced down the street. Hot tears fell from her eyes. She passed her neighbor Mrs. Diaz, and she turned her head away. She didn't want Mrs. Diaz to see that she was crying. Her neighbor gave Haley a sympathetic look, but Haley kept on running.

After a few blocks she felt a burning pain in her side. She stopped to catch her breath. She bent over with her hands on her knees, still crying. After a few moments she calmed down enough to look around.

She was near the park on Browndale Avenue, not far from Jill Wong's house. For a moment she considered going to Jill's. Then she remembered Jill wasn't there anymore. She wasn't even in Seneca Hills. She had returned to the Ice Academy in Denver.

Haley flushed, feeling foolish. She could go to Tori's house. Tori would understand. But Tori and her mom often went out to brunch on Sundays. Haley began walking slowly. She wasn't sure where she was headed. All she knew was that she couldn't go home.

Haley crossed the park, kicking a few leaves along the way. The trees were still bare, and there was a brisk breeze blowing. Haley sniffled. She wished she had a tissue, but her pockets were empty. When she reached the other side of the park, she realized that she wasn't far from Kathy's apartment building.

Kathy will understand, Haley thought. At least she cares about my skating. And Kathy understands how hard it is to skate and be responsible for school and everything else, too. My mother doesn't even *try* to see how tough things are for me.

Haley hurried to the brown brick building where Kathy lived. It was a cozy-looking place, with low hedges of holly bushes in the front yard. Haley rang the buzzer for Kathy's second-floor apartment. There was no answer.

Haley stepped back on the lawn and gazed up at Kathy's window. Her white curtains were open, and Haley could see that none of the lights were on. Haley walked around to the parking lot in the back. Kathy's tan Buick wasn't in her space.

Haley went slowly around to the building's entrance again. She sank onto the front steps. Maybe Kathy would be back soon. Haley wasn't sure what she would say to her coach when she did get back. But anything was better than facing her mother and sister.

I'm *never* going back there, Haley vowed. I'd rather walk all the way to Canada than go back to that house again!

9

An hour later, Haley was still sitting on Kathy's apartment steps. She was cold and miserable. But she was too upset and angry to go home. Finally Kathy's familiar car pulled around the corner of the park. Kathy slowed down at the driveway and waved to Haley.

Kathy looked surprised, Haley noted. Haley began to feel nervous. She hoped her coach wouldn't mind that she had shown up on her day off.

A moment later Kathy appeared carrying a bag of groceries in her arms. "Haley, what are you doing here?" she asked. "You look frozen! Have you been waiting long?"

Haley nodded. It was such a relief to feel that someone cared about her that for a moment she couldn't speak. There was a big lump in her throat, and she felt as if she was going to cry again.

"You seem upset," Kathy said. "Come on in. I'll make you some cocoa. All right?"

Haley tried to smile. "Thanks, Kathy," she mumbled, following her coach into the building.

"First, let's warm you up a little." Kathy set the grocery bag down on a counter in her apartment. She reached for a plaid wool blanket. "Give me your jacket and wrap up in this."

Haley pulled the blanket around her shoulders. Kathy hung her parka in the closet. Then she bustled around her kitchenette. "It'll just take a minute for the milk to heat up."

Haley sat on the blue-and-green-plaid couch. Soon Kathy brought in two steaming cups of hot chocolate. She set them on the glass coffee table and sat next to Haley on the couch.

"Okay," Kathy said. "Why don't you tell me what's going on. Is this about your trouble with the new skating routine?"

"No," Haley said, shaking her head. She felt tears start up again. "It's my parents," she began. "See, they've been fighting a whole lot lately. And now they've split up." The words started rushing out. "My dad just moved to Canada, and I don't even know when I'll see him again!" she wailed. "No one loves me anymore, and I never want to go back home!"

She started crying really hard. Kathy wrapped her arms around her. When Haley stopped crying, Kathy handed her a box of tissues. Haley wiped away some tears and blew her nose.

Kathy's eyes filled with concern. "I'm so sorry, Haley. This must be very hard for you."

Haley sniffled. "I hate it," she said. "The worst part is, nobody cares about me."

Kathy frowned. "It may seem that way to you now. But I'm sure it's not true," the coach insisted. "I know your parents care about you very much. But it's a big change to have someone leave the family."

"It's horrible," Haley agreed. "I can't believe my dad is really gone." She blew her nose again. "My mom just isn't interested in my skating. It was always my dad who cared about competitions and stuff. Now nobody cares at all."

"You may be closer to your dad," Kathy said. "But your mom's been to your competitions also. Maybe you're being too hard on her."

"No way," Haley said. "If she *really* cared about me, she'd let me visit my dad in Canada. But she said no."

"She said you could *never* visit him?" Kathy asked.

"Well, not exactly," Haley admitted. "Mostly she said it wasn't a good idea right now. But I bet she'll never think it's a good idea. She hates that I want to be with him."

Kathy narrowed her eyes. "Haley, does your mom know that you're here right now?"

Haley twisted her hands in her lap. "No," she answered. "We got into a big fight, and I ran out of the house."

"You'd better give her a call. She must be really worried about you," Kathy said.

"She *should* worry about me," Haley retorted. "Maybe then she'd care enough to let me go see my dad."

"I don't think that scaring her is a very good idea," Kathy said with a faint smile. "That won't convince her to let you go to Canada, will it?"

"Maybe not," Haley said.

Kathy handed her the phone. "Give her a call. I'll go make us more hot chocolate."

Haley punched in the number. Her mother answered on the first ring.

"Hi, Mom—" Haley said quickly.

Before she could get out another word, her mother interrupted. "Haley! Thank goodness! Are you all right? Where are you?"

"I'm okay, Mom. I'm at Kathy's," Haley replied.

"Haley, promise me that you won't *ever* run away again!" her mother cried. "I called all your friends, but no one knew where you were. I was so worried."

"Okay, I promise," Haley assured her mother.

"Haley, I've been thinking. Maybe it would be a good idea for you to visit your father."

"Really?" Haley asked. "You mean you're going to let me go?"

"Well, of course you can go at some point," her mother said.

"When?" Haley pushed.

"Why don't you come home? We'll talk it over."

"Okay," Haley agreed. "Kathy's making me more cocoa. I'll leave right after that."

"See you soon, Hals," her mother said.

Haley hung up the phone. She felt lots better already.

"I guess your mom was happy to hear from you, huh?" Kathy asked, coming back into the room. She sat on the sofa and rested her feet on the coffee table.

"You were right, Kathy. She was worried about me," Haley replied. "She even said we could talk about my visiting my dad."

"What part of Canada is he in?" Kathy asked.

"It's called Edmonton," Haley told her.

"Really? That's where they're holding the World Junior Championships!" Kathy gazed at Haley with excitement. "And they're during your spring break. You could go watch—it's a perfect time to visit."

Haley stared at Kathy in surprise. "That *would* be perfect!" she said.

"They have great rinks up there," Kathy told her. "You could get in some skating and not fall behind." Kathy was thoughtful for a moment. "As far as I'm concerned, it would be good for you. It might even help you out of the rut you and Patrick are in. Tell your mom what I said, okay?"

"Oh, Kathy, thank you!" Haley responded. "Is it hard to get tickets to the Worlds?"

"That's the last thing you should worry about. The important part is to talk to your mom and dad. But remember, the final decision is your mother's."

"I know. Oh, Kathy, I'm so lucky to have you as my coach!" Haley cried.

Kathy grinned. "That's what I'm here for. Do you want me to drive you home?" she asked.

"No, I'll walk. I can think about what to say to Mom on the way," Haley answered.

"Great," Kathy replied. "I'll see you in the morning."

Haley slipped on her parka. She hurried off, and soon she was back home.

"Haley, is that you?" her mother called from the kitchen.

"Yeah, Mom," Haley answered.

Mrs. Arthur hurried into the living room. She folded Haley into a big hug. "I'm so glad you're back," she said.

Haley snuggled against her mother's soft green sweater.

"All I could think of was how I could explain to your father if anything happened to you."

"I'm sorry, Mom. I was pretty upset," Haley told her.

"Well, I also realized how important it is for you to visit him. I'm sorry, too." Her mother squeezed her tighter.

"You mean I can go soon?" Haley asked.

"I mean we should talk about it. Let's sit down, okay?" Mrs. Arthur suggested.

She and her mom sat on the white couch.

"Mom, I was talking to Kathy, and she had a good idea," Haley began. "I mean, if it's okay with you. Because my spring break is coming up—"

"But that's only a week away!" Mrs. Arthur cut in. "Do you want to go that soon?"

"I wouldn't miss any school if I went then," Haley explained. "And there's something else." She took a deep breath. "The World Junior Championships are in

Edmonton. I could visit Dad and get a chance to see the championships. Kathy thinks it might be good for my skating," she added.

Her mother hesitated. "I wonder if your father would agree. Why don't I give him a call? Let's see what he has to say about it."

"Oh, Mom, thanks so much!" Haley exclaimed. "This is so exciting. I can't wait to go!"

10

Haley gazed out the window of the airplane. Below, she could see mountains covered with snow. Tori was curled up in the seat next to her under a navy-blue airline blanket, taking a nap. Haley's father had suggested that she bring a friend along. He would be busy at work a lot of the time. And Tori had been thrilled to accept.

It had been a long flight, but Haley was way too excited to sleep. She lifted a magazine from the pocket in front of her and began to leaf through it. She found an article titled "Edmonton, Shining City of the North."

The article explained that Canada didn't have states but provinces, which were much bigger. Edmonton was in western Canada. It was the capital of the province of Alberta. The 1988 Winter Olympics had been held there. Haley studied a picture of the huge Olympic stadium. Winter sports were very popular in Alberta.

People skied and tobogganed in the nearby mountains, and there were many skating rinks.

Haley began to daydream. She imagined herself a member of a prestigious Canadian skating club, working out at a beautiful rink. Her father would pick her up after practice, and they would go out for lasagna. Haley would tell him how her skating was going. It would be great to have her dad all to herself, she thought.

Tori yawned and stretched her arms. "Are we almost there?" she asked.

"I hope so," Haley said.

"I'm so excited," Tori told her. "We're going to have so much fun. I hope your dad really booked us skating time at a local rink."

"I'm sure he did," Haley told her. "And he's definitely getting us tickets for some of the World Juniors events, too."

Tori giggled. "Everyone in Silver Blades is so jealous!"

"Everyone but Patrick," Haley murmured. She and Patrick hadn't been getting along at all. Ever since their fight, things had been tense between them. Haley missed his friendship. And their skating had suffered, too. They still hadn't learned their new stomp-dance steps.

"Cheer up," Tori told her. "Think about everyone else. Not Patrick."

Haley sighed. "Okay. But it was tough telling everyone else about this trip, too. I had to explain why my dad is in Canada."

Haley had told the rest of her friends the truth about her father—that he wasn't living at home anymore. It hadn't been easy. But everyone had been really under-standing, Haley thought.

"Well, think of the good stuff," Tori said with a smile. "Like, no school for two whole weeks!"

"Ugh! Don't mention school!" Haley shuddered. "I have so much homework to make up. You know that detention Ms. Cantore gave me? The one I cut because I didn't want to miss practice? I have to do *two* detentions when I get back to make up for it."

"What a pain," Tori sympathized. "But at least we're going to have some fun first!"

"Yeah!" Haley agreed. And maybe I won't be going back to do that detention, she reminded herself. If I decide to stay in Canada, I'll be starting everything all over again. Even school.

Haley glanced at Tori and felt a pang of sadness. It wouldn't be easy to leave her friends if she did move in with her father. She wondered what Tori would think of the idea.

But just then a chime sounded. The FASTEN SEAT BELTS sign flashed on. The pilot's voice came over the speaker system. "Ladies and gentlemen, we are now beginning our descent into the Edmonton airport."

Haley shivered with excitement as she fumbled for her seat belt. This was it!

"My dad's the greatest," Haley said with excitement. "I can't wait to see his face when we get off the plane!"

A little while later, Haley and Tori left the long corridor that led from the airplane into the arrival area of the airport terminal. Haley scanned the crowd for her father. She spotted a family waiting with a homemade sign. It said WELCOME, GRANDMA. Nearby, a man and woman kissed hello.

"Where's your dad?" Tori asked.

Haley shrugged. "I guess he's late," she said. She tried not to feel disappointed.

"Look!" Tori pointed to a woman with dark hair. She wore a heavy black coat, and she was holding a white sign. HALEY ARTHUR was scrawled across it in big black letters.

Haley frowned. "Who do you think that is?"

"Let's find out," Tori suggested.

The two girls approached the woman. "Hi," Haley said. "I'm Haley Arthur."

"I'm glad to meet you, Haley. And you must be Tori," she said, shaking their hands. "I'm Wendy Benson, your father's assistant. He had a last-minute meeting, so he asked me to pick you up."

"Oh." Haley tried not to show her disappointment. She had really been looking forward to seeing her dad when she arrived. After all, she thought, *I* flew all the way to Canada to see *him*. Why couldn't *he* try harder to see *me*?

"Your dad said to tell you he's sorry. But he'll be home around dinnertime," Wendy assured Haley.

"Well, that's okay," she replied. "I guess I can wait a little longer to see him." She forced a smile.

"Let's go get your luggage. I'll drive you to your dad's apartment," Wendy said. "It's not too far. You must be tired after such a long trip."

Wendy led the way to the baggage claim. They spotted their suitcases, and Wendy helped carry them out to her car. As they drove, Haley gazed at the skyline. Edmonton had modern skyscrapers downtown. But the city was ringed by tall mountains. And the roads they drove on were lined with tall pine and fir trees.

"This doesn't feel so different from Seneca Hills," Haley remarked. "Though there's a lot more snow on the ground."

"Spring comes pretty late this far north," Wendy told her. "But you girls must like cold weather. Your dad says you're both terrific skaters."

"We both belong to an ice-skating club. It's called Silver Blades," Haley explained.

"I know. Your dad talks about you all the time," Wendy said. "In fact, he had me make lots of skating plans for you. You have skating time scheduled at the Alberta Ice Arena. I hear it's great. And you each have a two-day pass to the Junior World Championships."

"Super!" Haley and Tori exclaimed.

Wendy grinned. "They're for the pairs section. I know that Tori skates singles, but your dad thought you'd both like to see the pairs events."

"Oh. Is that okay, Tori?" Haley turned to her friend.

Tori frowned. "Well, I'm disappointed," she said. "But I guess it'll be okay."

Haley felt annoyed with Tori. But she didn't say anything.

"Here we are!" Wendy exclaimed. "Linden Street. This is the building. I have keys for you, and I'll give you your dad's number in case you need anything."

Haley glanced at the pretty apartment building. It was made of white stone and brick with a dark green awning over the front entrance. There were two urns with bushes on either side of the entryway. The heavy carved doors had large glass ovals set into their dark wood.

"Pretty fancy," Tori remarked.

"Here are the keys," Wendy told them. "It's number two-B. If you need anything, call the office."

"Wait," Haley said. "You're not going to stay with us till my dad gets here?"

Wendy frowned. "I really can't," she said. "I've got to get back to work."

Haley glanced uneasily around the empty lobby. She'd never been left alone in a strange place before.

She swallowed hard. "Um . . . thanks, Wendy," she managed to say.

Wendy smiled and waved as she left the building.

Haley glanced at Tori. No way would she act as if she was scared to be alone. She forced herself to act brave. After all, Dad will be here as soon as he can, she assured herself. And he probably can't wait to see me, either!

11

The lobby of the apartment building was brightly lit. It was decorated with gold mirrors and elegant green-and-white-striped wallpaper.

"This is so weird," Tori remarked. "We're staying at your dad's new place, and he's not even here."

"Yeah, well, he has some pretty important work to do," Haley answered.

Haley led Tori up a short flight of marble stairs. They found her dad's apartment right away. The door had an old-fashioned brass knocker on it. It was shaped like a lion's head with a ring in its mouth. Haley knocked, just to hear how it sounded. Then she used her key to open the door.

She and Tori set their stuff down on the hallway floor. The living room was large. But the only furniture was a big black leather couch and a matching pair of black end tables. Against one wall stood a floor-to-ceiling wall unit with a large-screen television.

"Hey, look!" Haley pointed at the television. "Pretty cool, huh?"

"It's huge!" Tori said.

"Yeah. It would be great to watch the Worlds on that. If we weren't going, that is," Haley joked. "Let's see what the rest of the place looks like. Then we can check out what's on TV."

The girls walked down the hallway. There were two doors at the end. One opened into the bathroom and the other into a bedroom painted light blue. There was a big double bed with a navy-blue comforter. Next to it stood a night table with a modern chrome lamp and a telephone. There was a picture of Haley and Morgan near the phone. Haley recognized the photo. It had been taken two Christmases before. She and her sister were sitting in front of the Christmas tree. She thought it was sweet that her father kept a picture of them near his bed.

"This must be his room," Haley said.

"Is that all there is, one bedroom?" Tori asked.

"I guess so," Haley answered. "After all, my dad is the only one living here."

"But where are we supposed to sleep?" Tori wondered.

"I guess we'll find out," Haley replied. "Let's see if there's anything to eat. I'm getting hungry."

"Me too," Tori said.

The girls went through the living room into a gleaming white kitchen. Haley opened the refrigerator. There were only some cans of soda and a loaf of bread. She opened the cabinets, but all she found were some crackers and a few cans of tomato paste.

"Well, he definitely needs to go shopping," Haley remarked. "How about crackers and a soda?"

"All right," Tori answered. "But I sure hope he brings something with him."

"Of course he will!" Haley exclaimed. "He probably doesn't do much cooking for himself."

"Unless he likes tomato paste sandwiches." Tori giggled.

Haley laughed. "Let's see what's on TV."

The girls settled in the living room. They flipped through the TV channels with the remote control.

"This is great!" Haley said. "There's Much Music, and some movie stations."

The girls spent the next couple of hours channel-surfing. They watched old movies for a while, then switched to music videos. Finally they settled on some cartoons. Just as Haley was starting to get bored, she heard a key in the lock.

She jumped up and ran to the door. Her father rushed in carrying a large pizza box. Haley threw her arms around him. "Hi, Dad!" she cried.

"Whoa, honey," her father said with a laugh. "I'm going to drop the pizza." He put the box down on a narrow table in the hallway and gave her a hug back. "How are you? Was the trip okay?"

"Great!" Haley answered. She carried the box of pizza into the living room.

"Mmm, smells good," she remarked, taking a deep whiff. "We're starved."

"Hello, Tori! Welcome to Canada," Mr. Arthur said. He hung his coat in the hall closet and unwrapped his wool scarf.

"Hi, Mr. Arthur," Tori greeted him.

"I hope mushroom and pepperoni is okay with you, Tori," Mr. Arthur said. He hung his suit jacket on the back of a chair. "It's Haley's and my favorite."

"It's great," Tori answered. "I love any kind of pizza."

"Me too," Haley agreed. "Mom never lets us have it for dinner. She doesn't think pizza is a well-balanced meal." She grinned at Tori. "Staying here is fun already!"

"I also picked up some movies at the video place," her dad told them. "And I brought some microwave popcorn."

"Great!" Haley declared. "I'll get us plates."

She hurried into the kitchen and got everything to set the table. She noticed that there were only two chairs.

"Dad, do you have another chair?" she asked.

"Nope, sorry," her father replied, scratching his chin. "Why don't you guys eat sitting on the couch? I'll pull one of these over." He dragged in a kitchen chair. "We'll have to camp out a little. I'm not really equipped for guests yet."

"No problem," Haley told him. She placed a slice of

pizza on a plate and handed it to Tori. She made plates for herself and her dad and sat down to eat.

"I've been so busy with work," Mr. Arthur explained. "I've hardly been here except to sleep and change my clothes. But it's a nice place, don't you think?"

"Very nice," Haley replied. But it's kind of small if I'm going to be staying here for good, she thought. She supposed her father would have to get a larger apartment if she moved in with him. One with a bedroom for her, too.

After dinner, Mr. Arthur made the popcorn and they settled down to watch the movies. Tori lay on the floor with her head on a throw pillow. Haley snuggled with her dad on the leather sofa.

Her father had rented two movies. One was called *Ice Dreams* and was all about skaters. The other was a horror film called *The Goblins*. Haley smiled to herself. Her dad had known just what movies she would like.

But by the end of the second movie, Haley realized that she was really tired. Tori looked pretty sleepy, too. She rubbed her eyes and yawned. Haley glanced at the clock.

"It's almost midnight!" she exclaimed. "Mom would *never* let us stay up this late." Still, she supposed they should get to bed.

"Dad, where are Tori and I going to sleep?" she asked.

"Oh, I guess we should make up your bed. I'm pretty tired myself," Mr. Arthur replied. "This couch is a sleeper. Now, where are those sheets?"

A few minutes later Mr. Arthur had found the sheets. Haley and Tori pulled open the couch and made up the bed together. Her dad pulled a fluffy down comforter and two pillows out of a closet. Haley and Tori brushed their teeth and got into their nightshirts. Mr. Arthur gave Haley a kiss good night.

"I hope you'll be comfortable, girls," Mr. Arthur said. He paused in the doorway. "See you in the morning."

Haley snuggled under the covers. She was so happy. It was great spending time with her dad in his new place. It was almost as good as having him back home. And at least here she didn't have to listen to any arguing.

Things were going so well—why should she leave?

Haley rolled over. "Tori?" she asked in a whisper. "Are you asleep?"

"Not yet," Tori answered. "What is it?"

"Tori, I've decided to move here with my dad," she confided. "You know, for good."

"Are you serious?" Tori sat bolt upright and stared at her in astonishment. "You mean, leave all your friends and everything?"

"I guess so," Haley said.

"Well, what about leaving your mother?" Tori asked.

"She won't care. Anyway, my dad cares more about me," Haley insisted.

"And what about your skating?" Tori frowned.

"I could skate here," Haley answered. "Maybe at the rink Wendy told us about. Anyway, my dad's the only one in my family who cares about my skating."

Tori seemed sad. "But Haley, I'd miss you so much if you moved up here."

"I know," Haley agreed. "I'd miss you, too. And Silver Blades, of course. But if I stay in Seneca Hills, I'll miss my dad."

"I still think you should be careful," Tori said slowly. "Remember when I thought I wanted to move? I was going to live with my father, too."

"I remember," Haley answered. A while ago, Tori had been fed up with her own mother. She'd decided to live with her father and her stepmother, Carol, in New York State. After she'd spent a little time with them, though, she'd changed her mind.

"But that was different, Tori," Haley pointed out. "You hardly even knew your father. And you didn't know Carol at all. My dad and I are really close. And it would just be the two of us."

"All I'm saying is that you should take your time. Really think about it," Tori advised. "After all, this is a pretty big decision."

"Believe me, I *have* been thinking about it," Haley said a little impatiently. Why couldn't Tori see things her way? "Living with my dad would be great, believe me," she insisted.

"Well, I just think you should be totally sure," Tori repeated.

Haley turned away and fluffed up her pillow. She didn't want Tori to see how angry she felt. After all, Tori was her best friend. She should be on Haley's side. Why couldn't she see that living with her dad would be the best thing for Haley?

After a few minutes, Haley could hear Tori's even breathing. Haley snuggled under the covers. She stared up at the ceiling in the dark. She remembered the photograph of Morgan and herself on her father's nightstand. We were so happy back then, she thought. No wonder he likes to look at it before he goes to sleep.

It could be like that again if I lived here. It wouldn't be like having the whole family together, but . . . Suddenly Haley smiled. Living with her father alone would be even *better*! Because that way she'd have him all to herself.

12

"**H**aley, wake up," Mr. Arthur said, gently shaking her shoulder.

Haley opened her eyes with a start and looked up at her father. She glanced over at Tori, asleep next to her. Haley rubbed her eyes and sat up, feeling grumpy.

"What time is it?" she mumbled. "I feel like I just fell asleep."

"Early. Five-thirty," he answered.

Haley let herself fall back on the bed. She closed her eyes again. "But it's vacation. Why are you waking me up so early?" She moaned.

"You want to go skating, right?" he asked, shaking her shoulder again. "I have a meeting, and the rink is pretty far away. We've got to get going or I'll never meet my client in time."

"Okay, okay. But why did you let us stay up so late

if you knew we had to get up this early?" Haley asked with a scowl.

"I'm not used to thinking about stuff like that. I figured you knew what you were doing," her father replied. "I guess we're going to have to plan a little better."

"I guess so," said Haley sleepily. She turned to Tori and gave her friend a nudge. "Tori. Get up."

"Okay," Tori mumbled, without moving.

"*Tori*," Haley said, getting out of bed. "We have to get up."

"I heard you the first time," Tori growled.

"Come on," Haley said, pulling on Tori's arm to try to drag her out of the bed. Haley started to laugh. "I'm not carrying you to the rink. Get up." She pulled harder, and Tori fell to the floor with a thump. Tori kept her eyes closed, but Haley could tell that she was trying not to laugh.

Tori's eyes fluttered open. "Okay, I think I'm up now," she said. They both laughed. "What time is it, anyway?"

"Early. But my dad has a meeting, and he has to drive us to the rink now," Haley explained.

"Okay," Tori replied. "Do we get to eat something?"

"Dad!" Haley called out. "What about breakfast?"

"Oh, yeah," her father said, coming into the room while he knotted his tie. "How about some donuts? We can stop on the way."

Donuts? thought Haley. Donuts were all right for a Sunday, but not for a skating day. "Dad, you're going to have to go shopping soon," she told her father. "It takes a lot of energy to skate. We need something better than donuts, okay?"

"I'll try, I promise. Now, why don't you get dressed? We've got to get moving," her father answered, ruffling her hair.

Haley walked into the bathroom. She splashed some cold water on her face and brushed her teeth. Looking in the mirror, she saw that she looked about as tired as she felt. I wish we hadn't stayed up so late, she thought. Tonight it's going to be an early night, she promised herself.

Fifteen minutes later, the girls and Mr. Arthur got in the car. Haley sat up front with her father and Tori sat in the back. Haley gazed curiously at the houses and neighborhoods they passed on the way to the donut shop. The houses here were set very far apart. And the mountains were all around them. It's pretty, she thought. I could like living here.

They pulled up to a mini-mall across from the freeway entrance. The sign read OLYMPIC DONUTS and had five donuts linked together like the five rings of the Olympic symbol.

"You picked this place on purpose, didn't you, Dad?" Haley asked with a grin, pointing at the sign.

Mr. Arthur smiled. "I thought you'd get a kick out of it," he offered. "I always stop here for my coffee. It makes me think of you, champ."

Haley smiled happily. The three of them hurried into the shop. Haley gazed at the display case crammed with sugary donuts. Dad's going to have to change his eating habits, Haley thought. Pizza and donuts are great treats. But they're not a good diet for an athlete.

Mr. Arthur bought the girls their donuts and some orange juice and got himself an extra-large coffee. They sat at the counter, eating breakfast.

"So, Mr. Arthur, how big is the ice arena here?" Tori asked, perking up a bit.

"I'm not really sure," he answered.

"Do you know if there's more than one rink, like we have at home?" Haley asked.

"To tell you the truth, Wendy made the arrangements for me. I never spoke to anyone over there. But you'll know soon enough," he said cheerfully. "It's been so hectic getting used to the new office, I haven't had time to do anything else. But skating pros like you are going to have a blast, I'm sure."

Haley knew her dad meant well. Still, she wished he'd spent more time thinking about her.

"Is it far to the rink from here?" she asked.

"Pretty far. I can drive you guys there this morning. But I'll show you where the bus stops. You'll have to get there by yourselves tomorrow," her father answered.

"By ourselves?" Haley repeated. "Can't you just take us?"

"I wish I could, Haley, but it's out of the way. I can't make the trip every day. But look, the bus stop is right over there," he said. He pointed across the street to a bench near the freeway entrance. "I can bring you here with me in the morning. When you come home, you make a transfer here to the green line. It stops two blocks from the house. It's a long ride, but you have plenty of time. It's not like you have to do this every day, right?"

"Oh," Haley said. "Right."

She forced a smile. If she lived here, though, she *would* have to do it every day. And she'd practically have to get up in the middle of the night to make it to a skating session before school! She glanced over at Tori, who raised her eyebrows.

Mr. Arthur glanced at his watch and frowned. "Better get hopping," he said. "It's a long drive to the rink. And I can't be late to my meeting."

Haley gulped down the rest of her chocolate donut. "Sure, Dad. Okay."

Half an hour later they pulled into the parking lot of a huge round building. The words ALBERTA ICE ARENA were spelled out in giant red letters across the front. The mountains and the clear blue sky were reflected in mirrored windows that circled the upper floors of the building. Mr. Arthur turned to Haley with a grin.

"Big enough for you, Hals?" he asked.

"Wow! This looks fantastic!" Haley cried.

"It's incredible," Tori gushed. "It's even bigger than the Lake Placid Arena. Remember when we competed at the Regionals there, Haley? Don't you think this is bigger?"

"Definitely," Haley responded.

"Well, have lots of fun, girls," Mr. Arthur said. "Check

in at the desk. They'll set you up with lockers. If you need anything, call the office. I'll be in meetings all day, but Wendy can help you out."

"Thanks, Dad," Haley said, opening the car door.

Haley and Tori jumped out of the car and waved as Mr. Arthur drove off. They hurried through the big swinging glass doors. Haley spotted a reception desk in the front part of the lobby. To the right, she saw a balcony with a white metal railing.

"Come on, let's take a look over that balcony before we check in," Haley said.

"Okay," Tori agreed.

They leaned over the railing. The balcony hung about thirty feet above the next level. The ground floor had a little plaza area with trees and café tables in front of an Olympic-sized rink. Looking up, Haley saw skylights and more balconies on the two floors above them.

Haley gasped. "This is even bigger than it looks from the outside," she said. "What do you think they have up there?" she asked, pointing to the upper levels.

"More rinks?" Tori guessed. "Let's find out."

They walked back to the reception desk. The desk was surrounded by a row of small trees in pretty blue pots and a large red painting with yellow squiggles on it. A tall blond man wearing a green pullover stood at the desk, talking on the phone. He hung up and turned to Haley and Tori.

"May I help you?" he asked.

"My name's Haley Arthur, and this is Tori Carsen," Haley said. "We're supposed to have skate time today."

"Oh, yes," the man confirmed. "I have your reservations right here. And your rink time is already paid for." He paused. "You're from Silver Blades in Seneca Hills, right?" he asked.

"That's right," said Haley. "We're just visiting." For *now* I'm just visiting, she added silently. She felt a burst of pride, thinking that this could be her rink soon.

"My name is Todd Burns," said the man. "I'll show you the rink where the freestyle sessions will be."

Todd signaled to a woman to take his place at the desk. "Follow me," he said to Haley and Tori. "I'll give you a tour. We have four rinks, a weight-training room, a sauna and steam rooms, and dance studios." He led them down the stairs.

"This is awesome," Tori murmured. Haley could see she was really impressed.

"I'm glad you like it," Todd replied. "I'm a skater myself, and I always feel lucky to be able to skate here."

They stopped in the central courtyard. Todd pointed to a hallway. "Down there is a snack bar. You can eat in the plaza if you like. Let me show you the locker rooms."

They started to circle the rink they had seen from upstairs. There were a few skaters already working out on the ice.

"You'll be skating in this rink," Todd said, pointing to the gleaming ice. "We have a few other skaters booked for today, but you'll have plenty of room. There's another rink on this level, and two smaller ones on the floor above us. The sauna and steam rooms are down here, too. The top floors have the weight-training and dance studios. Feel free to use the sauna or steam, if you like."

"Wow, that sounds great," Haley replied. "We don't have that in Seneca Hills."

"Oh, it's wonderful," Todd commented. "Very relaxing after a tough workout."

He pointed down the hallway. "There you are. The women's locker room. There are towels at the desk in the shower area. If there's anything else you need, let me know." He turned back toward the plaza.

"Thanks, Todd," Haley said.

"You're welcome. Have fun!" Todd hurried back upstairs.

Haley pushed open the door. The locker room was as big and fancy as every other part of the arena. It had beige carpeting, pale wood lockers, and lighted mirrors on the walls. Haley and Tori exchanged excited glances.

"Wait till everyone at Silver Blades hears about this," Tori cried.

"I can't wait to tell them," Haley agreed.

Tori frowned. "But you won't be going back to tell them," she reminded Haley.

Haley blinked. "Oh. Right," she murmured. "I almost forgot."

Suddenly she had a funny feeling in her stomach. But she turned and flashed Tori a big smile.

"Well, this place is tons better than the Seneca Hills rink," Haley declared. "And I can't wait to practice here every day!"

13

Haley and Tori changed quickly. Haley pulled out her new outfit. Her mom had bought it as a special surprise right before Haley left on her trip. It was a bright blue unitard with lighter blue designs all over. It brought out the red in Haley's hair and made her brown eyes seem to sparkle more brightly than ever.

"Cool outfit!" Tori cried.

"Thanks," Haley said, feeling pleased.

Tori slipped into a pale pink velvet skating dress trimmed with ivory lace.

"Hey, Tori." Haley frowned, glancing at her friend's outfit. "What happened? Didn't you bring your good skating clothes with you?"

Tori stared down at her skating dress. "But this is brand-new! My mom just made it for me, and—"

Haley burst out laughing. "Calm down," she said. "I was kidding. That dress is incredible. You look like you just stepped out of a fairy tale."

"Good," Tori said. She gave herself a satisfied smile in the mirror and fixed her hair.

The girls slipped on their skate guards and light blue Silver Blades warm-up jackets and hurried to the rink. It was brightly lit. The huge glass panels showed the pink and gold light of the sunrise.

Haley began her off-ice warm-up. Three other skaters were already practicing. Two were pairs skaters going through a routine. The boy had light brown hair and smiled a lot as he skated. The girl wore navy-blue leggings with a beige sweater. Her dark brown hair was pulled back in a French twist. The third skater was a tall, good-looking boy. He had black hair and olive skin.

Haley started stretching, but she watched the pairs couple out of the corner of her eye.

"What do you think?" Tori whispered, indicating the other skaters with her chin. She leaned over to stretch her hamstrings.

"They look pretty good," Haley answered, watching more intently.

The girl smiled at her partner as they moved into a spiral combination. They jumped into a series of Arabian cartwheels. They were definitely good.

Haley glanced at the single boy skater. He noticed her watching and did a few crossovers in his end of the ice. Then he leaped into a tight double axel followed by a triple toe loop. He had a lot of upper-leg strength, Haley noticed. His takeoff and landing were smooth.

"What about him?" Tori asked quietly. "He's very strong. And pretty cute, too."

"He's at least as good as Patrick," Haley agreed.

"Looks like he's coming over," Tori added under her breath.

The dark-haired boy glided up to Haley and Tori. He was several inches taller than Patrick, Haley noted.

"Hi," he said. "I'm Matt. I've never seen you here before."

"We don't live here," Haley answered. "We're from Pennsylvania. I'm Haley, and this is my friend Tori."

"Oh, Americans. Great! Welcome to Canada," he replied with a grin. "It's a pretty nice rink, eh?"

"Definitely." Haley grinned back. "We're from a club called Silver Blades."

"Silver Blades? I've heard of it." Matt's eyes twinkled with interest. "That's a top club, isn't it? Are you both singles skaters?" he asked.

"I am," Tori told him.

"Too bad," Matt said. "I'm a pairs skater myself."

"You are?" Haley smiled in surprise. "So am I!"

"Really?" Matt seemed pleased. "I happen to be in between partners right now," he answered. "You want to see if we can practice together? Unless you'd rather hang out with your friend," he said, glancing at Tori.

"Don't worry about me," Tori said quickly. "Like I said, I skate singles. But Haley's one of the best pairs skaters in Silver Blades," she bragged to Matt.

"One of the best, eh?" He grinned. "Let's see if you can prove it."

"I always accept a challenge," Haley replied with a laugh. "You're on."

Haley and Matt glided away from the boards and put some distance between themselves.

"All right, Miss America," Matt teased. "Let's try some side-by-side jumps?"

"No problem," Haley replied with a grin. "How about a double axel, double toe loop, and spread eagle combination?"

"You've got it," Matt responded.

Watching each other carefully, Haley and Matt began circling the rink. After a series of crossovers, they gave each other a nod and lifted into the double axel–double toe loop combination. They landed at almost the exact same time. They circled each other in spread eagles. They glided closer together.

Matt did a half turn so that he was facing Haley while skating backward. "How about some spins?" he suggested.

Haley quickly agreed. It would be too dangerous to practice any lifts with a brand-new partner. But they could easily—and safely—try some side-by-side sit spins.

"How about sit spins, side-by-side double flips, side-by-side double axels, and side-by-side sit spins again?" she said.

Matt grinned in reply. He glided into back crossovers, and Haley did the same. They stepped in the same direction on the entrance edge. They began the spins at exactly the same moment. They finished the sit spins facing the same way and moved easily into an upright position for another set of crossovers.

They each glided easily into the double flip and landed perfectly. They rose into impressive double axels and into back crossovers again. They ended the routine with another pair of perfectly matched sit spins.

Haley stood up and waited with her hands on her hips. Matt glided over to her and they gave each other a high five. Then they skated back to the boards, where Tori was watching.

"You guys were *great* together!" Tori said. Her eyes were wide with surprise.

"It was fun," Haley agreed. Her heart was fluttering with excitement. Matt was an incredible match for her.

"That was great!" Matt exclaimed with a huge grin. "You're as good as your friend said, Haley."

"Hey, Matt!" Haley heard someone call. The pairs skaters she had noticed earlier glided up to the boards next to them.

"Hi, guys," Matt greeted them.

"Hi!" The girl grinned at Haley. "I'm Céline Bonnard. That was some nice skating."

"Thanks," Haley replied. "I'm Haley Arthur. And this is my friend Tori Carsen."

"Hi, Tori," Céline said. "This is my partner, Jacques Benning," she added, indicating the boy behind her.

"*Salut*," Jacques said with a French-sounding accent. His green eyes sparkled under a fringe of brown bangs. "Nice to meet you both," he added.

"Are you French Canadian?" Tori asked.

"Yes. From Québec," Céline explained. "In that part of Canada, French is the first language."

Haley realized that Céline also had an accent, but it was not nearly as strong as Jacques's.

"Are you Americans?" Jacques asked.

"Sure are," Haley said.

"We're from Pennsylvania," Tori added.

"They're in Silver Blades," Matt told the others.

"Really? But what brings you to Edmonton? Are you skating in the championships?" Céline asked, puzzled.

"I wish!" Haley declared. "We're visiting my father. But we're going to watch some of the Worlds."

"Céline and Jacques are skating tomorrow," Matt told her. "They're one of the top pairs in Canada."

"Wow, that's great!" Haley was impressed. "You must be so excited."

"Very," Céline said. "But a little nervous, too."

"That's why we were practicing so hard just now," added Jacques.

"Actually, we'd better get back to work," Céline said, gesturing to Jacques to join her. "See you later." She gave Haley and Matt a smile before she and Jacques skated off together.

"I'd better start skating, too," Tori said. "See you in a while, Haley." She glided to a far corner of the rink.

"So, what do you think, Haley? Want to skate some

more?" Matt asked. "I think we make a pretty good pair."

Haley had to agree. They certainly seemed to skate well together. "Okay, let's try some more," she said.

They skated to a corner of the rink. "I'm going to the Worlds tomorrow, too," Matt told her. "Why don't we watch the pairs competition together?"

"Sure. That sounds great," Haley agreed.

"All right, Miss America. Let's try those moves again, okay?" Matt grinned.

"You're on!" Haley said.

Matt was incredible. He was really cute. Almost as cute as Alex, Haley thought. Plus Matt was a terrific skater. And he gave Haley tons of praise. He wasn't critical and picky, the way Patrick had been lately. Skating with him made Haley feel good about herself again. And that was a feeling she wanted to hold on to.

14

"That was the best!" Haley cried. She was full of excitement about the day at the rink. She dropped her parka on the floor of her father's apartment and flopped down on the black leather couch.

"I had a blast today," Tori agreed.

"Wasn't that steam room great?" Haley asked. "Todd was right. It felt fantastic after a hard workout."

"You and Matt had a great session," Tori said. "You guys were incredible together. It really seemed like you had skated together before."

"Yeah, he was terrific," Haley agreed.

"But now I'm starving. Are you?" Tori asked.

Haley's stomach growled. She and Tori laughed. "I guess so," Haley said. "I hope Dad comes home soon."

Haley and Tori had eaten lunch with Matt, Céline, and Jacques at the snack bar at the rink. But that had been hours ago. The trip home on two buses had taken a long time. Haley was hungry again.

Tori jumped up. "Maybe we missed something in the kitchen."

"I'm pretty sure there's nothing in there," Haley called after her.

Haley reached for the remote and turned on the TV. She leaned back on the couch. The blankets and pillows from the night before were still piled there. Haley snuggled up with a pillow. A moment later Tori returned from the kitchen.

"You're right," said Tori. "Nothing. Maybe we can go out and grab something."

"I haven't seen any stores around here. Have you?" Haley asked.

"I guess not." Tori sounded disappointed. She plunked down next to Haley. "I hope your dad brings home a lot of food," she grumbled.

Haley glanced at her. Why did Tori have to be so grouchy? Haley knew that Tori was hungry, but she was hungry, too. "I'm sure Dad will be home early tonight," she said.

Haley flipped through the channels. There wasn't much on that she was interested in. Finally she stopped at a music video. "How's this?"

"Okay, I guess." Tori sighed.

Three hours went by. Haley had long since gotten bored with television. She sprawled on the floor with her math book, making up some of her missed assignments. Tori was flipping through a magazine she had bought in the airport. When Mr. Arthur finally walked in the door, it was seven o'clock.

"Dad! You're home!" Haley cried in relief. At least her father had some bags in his arms. "What's for dinner? We're starved," she said.

"No problem!" Her dad began to pull fast-food boxes from the bags. "Look—Chicken Express! They make the best fried chicken. I got drumsticks and wings."

More junk food? Haley thought. "Uh, great," she said, trying to sound enthusiastic. A steady diet of this food wasn't nutritious enough for skating. Haley's mother was a great cook, and Haley was used to her home-cooked meals. She wondered what her mother and Morgan were eating that night. Probably something healthy *and* delicious, like pasta with vegetables and chicken, she thought.

"So, how was skating today, girls?" Haley's father asked.

"It was great, Dad," Haley answered. "That arena is amazing."

"They have four rinks there," Tori added. "And weight rooms and a dance studio and everything. It's going to be tough going back to the Seneca Hills arena after this."

"Really," Haley agreed. She and Tori exchanged quick glances. Haley could tell that Tori was wondering when Haley was going to tell her dad that she wasn't going back.

She gave Tori a shrug to let her know that she was still thinking about it.

They sat down to eat. Mr. Arthur gazed around the crowded living room. "Boy, this place is a mess," he said. "Didn't you girls have time to straighten up today?"

Haley glanced around the room. Clothing was piled all over the place. "There's no place to unpack," Haley told her dad.

Mr. Arthur sighed. "Guess not," he agreed. He had dropped his briefcase in the middle of the living room. And there were stacks of his papers on the table in the entryway and on the wall unit opposite the couch. At home, Haley's room was usually pretty messy. But her mother made sure the rest of the house stayed nice.

"So, Dad, what are we doing tonight?" Haley asked.

"What about a movie or something?" Tori suggested.

"I can't go anywhere tonight," her father answered. "I've got to get ready for a big meeting." He bit into his chicken.

Haley sighed. If she'd been at home, she could have asked her mom to drop her and Tori at the mall. They could have gone to a movie or done some shopping.

"Could Tori and I go someplace by ourselves?" Haley asked.

"Well, the movies are pretty far away. And I've got to get right to work. I'm sorry," her dad apologized. "There's probably something on TV."

"Not more TV!" Tori groaned.

Haley tried to hide her disappointment.

The telephone rang. Mr. Arthur hurried to answer it. "Oh, hi," he said. "Yes, she's right here." He waved Haley to the phone. "It's Mom," he told her, handing her the receiver.

"Hi, Mom," Haley said into the phone.

"Hi! How's it going, sweetheart?" her mother asked. "Is everything okay?"

"Great, Mom," Haley answered with a little more enthusiasm than she felt. She felt a sudden pang of homesickness. She wondered what her mother and Morgan were doing that night.

"We went skating today, and you wouldn't believe how great the rink was," Haley continued.

"That's wonderful," her mother said. "I'm glad you're having a good time. Morgan and I are having fun, too. But I miss you a lot."

"I miss you, too, Mom," Haley answered. As she said it, she realized that it was true. Things had been rough between her and her mother lately. But being away made Haley remember a lot of the good things about home.

"Are you sure you're okay?" her mother asked again. "Everything's going well?"

"Great, Mom. Really," Haley assured her. "We're so tired that we decided to stay in and take it easy tonight." Haley tried to sound as if they were thrilled to stay in and watch TV again.

"Well, Morgan wants to say hello," her mother remarked. "I'll put her on."

Morgan's voice came on the line. "Haley, guess what? Mom and I are going to the Mid-Atlantic Horse Show tomorrow! Isn't that great?"

Haley felt a wave of jealousy. Mom and Morgan are having a great time without me, she thought. I bet they don't miss me at all.

"We're doing lots of things with Dad, too," Haley fibbed. "And the World Junior Championships start tomorrow. Tori and I met some of the top skaters in Canada today. They said we were great skaters, too," she bragged.

"Oh," Morgan said. "That's nice."

"Yeah, we're having a great time," Haley continued. "Dad's so happy I'm here."

"Oh, hang on a sec," Morgan told her. "Mom wants to say something else."

Mrs. Arthur got back on the phone. "I just wanted to say good night. I love you, sweetheart," she added gently.

"I love you, too, Mom," Haley replied. Suddenly she felt a little choked up.

"Bye, honey." Her mother hung up.

Haley put down the receiver. She felt tears in her throat for the first time that day. But she forced a smile and turned around. Tori was sitting alone on the couch.

"Where's my dad?" Haley asked.

"He went into his room to work," Tori answered. "Are you okay? You seem kind of upset."

"I'm not sure," Haley answered.

She didn't want to admit that she was mad at her father. She understood that he had to work. But she couldn't help wishing that he would spend time with her instead.

"I guess I'm kind of confused," Haley finally said. "I thought I wanted to stay here with my dad. But now I'm not so sure."

"Well, if you ask me, things aren't so great here," Tori blurted out. "I mean, don't get me wrong. I'm really happy I came and everything. But if it were up to me, I wouldn't want to live here. Your dad's nice, but he's always so busy. It seems like he can't think about anything but work."

"Well, he just moved here, after all. Things will be different when he's really settled," Haley said in her father's defense.

"Still, you'd be on your own a lot. More than in Seneca Hills," Tori pointed out.

"That could be good, though. I mean, there'd be less rules and stuff," Haley retorted. "And you have to admit that the Alberta Ice Arena is fantastic."

"Oh, definitely. And that guy Matt seems like a perfect partner for you," Tori added. "Plus he's really cute."

Haley smiled. Leave it to Tori to say something like that! "Well, he's a great skater, and it's the skating that counts."

Tori rolled her eyes. "Haley, you always say that!" Haley and Tori both laughed.

"Of course," Tori went on, "Alex is really cute, too."

"Yeah." Haley blushed at the mention of Alex's name. *If I move to Canada I'll never get to have that date with him*, she realized.

"So, what about Matt?" asked Tori. "Are we meeting him at the Worlds tomorrow?"

"Yeah. Downstairs in the lobby," Haley answered. "It's going to be so much fun. I can't wait to see Céline and Jacques skate in an important competition."

"Me too," Tori agreed. "So, you want to watch some TV?"

"I guess so," Haley said.

The girls turned the television back on, but there wasn't much that Haley really wanted to watch. She felt bored and a little sad. She remembered that she had promised herself an early night.

"Tori, I'm getting tired," Haley announced.

"So am I," Tori admitted. "Let's go to sleep."

Haley changed into her nightshirt and went to brush her teeth in the bathroom. As she passed her father's room she noticed a light shining underneath his door.

I'll say good night after I brush my teeth, she decided.

A few minutes later she knocked on the door, but there was no answer. She cracked the door open and peered inside. Her dad had fallen asleep with his clothes on. Papers were spread all around him on the bed.

Wow, he really *has* been working hard, Haley realized. She thought about waking him up, but decided to let him sleep. She didn't want to disturb him.

Besides, she needed to get some sleep, too. She and Tori had to be up early the next day for the Worlds. She could hardly wait!

15

❧❧❧

The next morning Haley woke up bright and early. It was the first time she'd slept well in a week. She bounced out of bed and went to wash up. She grinned at herself in the bathroom mirror. Today we're going to the World Junior Championships! she thought happily.

The Worlds competition was one of the most important in a skater's career. Haley dreamed of competing there someday. The best skaters from every country competed. Winning a medal at the Worlds was a top honor.

Haley thought of Céline with a pang of envy. This competition could be a big break for her and Jacques. Maybe Haley could compete as a junior in the Nationals next year. Tori and Amber had done well there this year. If Haley made it to the Nationals, it would be an important step in her career. And then, someday, she might make it to the Worlds!

Haley hurried into the living room. She bounced onto the sofa bed.

"Come on, Tori! Time to get up!" she cried.

"Okay, okay," Tori said. She sat up, rubbing her eyes and then stretching. "I'm getting dressed." Tori closed her eyes again, lay back down, and rolled over.

Haley grinned mischievously. She grabbed a pillow, swung it over her head, and smashed it down on Tori. Tori gave a squeal and leaped up with her own pillow. They laughed and shrieked, hitting each other with the pillows until they collapsed in a fit of giggles.

Mr. Arthur emerged from his room and grinned at them. "Are you ready yet? We have to leave in ten minutes."

An hour later, Haley and Tori found themselves in the Olympic Sports Center. The enormous lobby was hung with flags of countries from around the world.

She was thrilled to stand where so many Olympic hopefuls had been. Some had gone on to make Olympic history.

"This is so exciting," Haley whispered to Tori.

"It's totally awesome," Tori agreed, gazing around the cavernous space. "Let me take a picture of you, and then you can take a picture of me," she suggested.

She handed Haley her camera. Haley spotted a large statue of a man and a woman standing underneath a golden Olympic torch. She pointed to the sculpture. "How about over there?"

As they hurried to the sculpture, Haley heard a familiar voice behind her.

"Why don't I take one of the two of you together?"

Haley whirled around. Matt!

"Good timing," she replied with a grin.

"Timing is everything," Matt shot back.

Matt snapped the picture of Haley and Tori. Then Tori took one of Haley and Matt together.

"Okay, enough pictures," Matt said. "Let's find our seats inside."

"I can't wait to see Céline and Jacques compete," Haley remarked as they hurried through the lobby. "Have they been together very long?"

"Four years," Matt answered. "Actually, Céline and I skated together a few times. That was before she paired up with Jacques." Matt grinned at Haley. "But we didn't have that special chemistry together. Sometimes you know right away when something's perfect."

Haley flushed. Was Matt really hinting that he'd like to be her partner? Or something more?

Matt, Haley, and Tori found good seats near the boards. The skating order was announced. Céline and Jacques would be the second pair to skate their short program.

The short programs all contained the same elements. The pairs were judged on technical and artistic merit. The judges would pay special attention to their jumps, side-by-side performances, and spiral combinations.

The first set of skaters was from Argentina. They wore matching red outfits with black fringe on the sleeves. They seemed comfortable together and did well on their technical scores. But their marks for artistic impression weren't nearly as high. Their overall score was average.

"They'll have to do better than that in the long program if they want to place well," Tori commented.

The long programs would be the next day. Most skaters put a lot of effort into choosing their routines. They could put together their choice of moves in a way that showed off their special skills. The skating order for the long programs would be determined by how well the skaters placed in the short program the first day.

"There are Céline and Jacques," Matt announced. "They look pretty relaxed, eh?" He nodded in approval.

Haley crossed her fingers for her new Canadian friends. Céline and Jacques glided onto the middle of the ice. They looked terrific in matching navy-blue outfits with white trim. They smiled to the crowd, and Jacques winked at Céline.

They waited for their music to start. Haley noted Céline's perfect posture, with a long spine and extended neck.

Haley imagined herself as a Canadian skater with Matt as her partner. She frowned. Matt was right, she thought! It was special to find that magic with a skating partner. All the great pairs skaters said the same thing. Haley had felt it when she first skated with Patrick. She wondered if she and Patrick still had that special quality. Or had their big fight changed everything?

The music started, and Haley forgot about everything else as Céline and Jacques launched into their double loop jumps. The pair completed a flawless double twist. They did their pairs spin combination and glided into the spiral step sequence. Their performance was smooth and relaxed. Haley admired their style and control. The final required move was a toe lasso, and Haley paid special attention. Céline and Jacques performed it elegantly and with a lot of strength. Jacques lifted Céline as though it were effortless, and she kept a graceful position with clean lines throughout the lift. There was a round of applause at the end of their program.

The judges gave them high scores for both the technical and artistic elements of the program.

"I'm going to run down and get a picture of them," Tori announced. She grabbed her camera. "Be back in a minute."

"Céline and Jacques are the pair to beat," Matt remarked when Tori left. "I'm happy for them." He turned to Haley with a serious expression. "But I'd be happier skating there myself. We could be a good pairs team, Haley. Don't you think so?"

Haley hesitated. "I *have* been thinking about it," she admitted. "But, you know, I'd have to move to Canada, and—"

"And that's a big deal," Matt finished for her. "I know. But you seem to like it up here. And I'm looking for a partner." He shrugged and flashed her a bright smile.

Haley smiled back. It felt great that Matt wanted to skate with her.

Moments later Tori returned. Haley glanced at her, anxious to tell her about Matt's offer. But Haley remembered Tori's warnings about moving to Canada. She decided not to mention it for now.

The pairs short program ended with Céline and Jacques in first place.

"Let's go congratulate them," Matt suggested.

The three of them rushed down to the boards. Céline waved them over excitedly.

"Congratulations," Haley cried, giving her new friend a hug. "You guys were great!"

"*Merci*—thank you. I'm so glad you could be here!" Céline said happily. "But it's not over yet. Oh, I almost forgot. I have a surprise for all of you!"

"What's that?" Matt asked.

"Jacques and I got extra passes for tonight's big opening-night party. It's held here, at the arena. You'll be my guests!" Céline exclaimed.

"Wow, thanks," Haley said.

"Sounds like a blast!" Matt agreed.

Tori nodded in agreement. "Who's going to be there?" she asked.

"Just about everybody," Céline told her. "We all invite friends and family. It starts right after the last event. It makes it a pretty long day."

"That's okay. A party sounds great!" Haley exclaimed. "I'd better call my dad, though. What time should I tell him to pick us up?" she asked.

"Nine o'clock should be right," Céline suggested. "It

ends pretty early, since everyone has to be fresh to skate tomorrow. I'll leave then, too."

"Oh!" Tori cried. "What about clothes? We didn't bring anything to party in." Tori gazed down at her outfit. She was wearing slim black pants with an oversized turquoise sweater. Haley was wearing dark leggings and a wildly patterned tunic top.

"You both look great," Céline assured Tori and Haley. "But I have some extra clip-on earrings and things in my skate bag. And we can fix your hair really special. It's not a fancy party, anyway."

"Sounds perfect, then," Tori said, with a smile of relief.

Haley gazed happily from Céline to Matt to Tori. The party was going to be so much fun!

Later that evening, Haley, Tori, Matt, Céline, and Jacques sat at their own table at the party. Céline had arranged Tori's hair into a sophisticated French twist. She had lent Haley a pair of huge gold hoop earrings. Haley thought she and Tori looked terrific. At the party, all of them had piled their plates high with incredible food. They dug in, starving after the exciting but long day of watching skating events.

In the center of the room a dance floor was set up. A deejay played upbeat rock tunes.

"Mmm," Tori murmured, taking another bite of the

shrimp on her plate. "This sure beats Chicken Express!"

"What?" Jacques asked.

"Never mind," Haley told him.

Tori gazed around the room. "Wow," she said. "Everywhere you look, there's an amazing skater or coach." She nudged Haley in the ribs. "Isn't that Elvis Stojko?" she asked.

Everyone turned to catch a glimpse of the famous Canadian figure skater. He was dancing in the center of the room and really kicking up a storm.

"He's as wild on the dance floor as he is on the ice." Tori giggled.

"This is so exciting!" Haley cried. She turned to Céline. "Thanks so much for asking us."

"No problem," Céline answered.

Matt threw his napkin onto the table and turned to Haley. "Let's show Elvis how wild we can be," he said.

Haley glanced at Tori. She didn't want to leave Tori alone.

"Go ahead," Tori told her. "I'll be fine."

"Okay, let's go!" Haley declared.

Matt and Haley threaded their way through the tables to the dance floor. A mirrored ball hung from the high ceiling overhead. It cast flashing reflections over the crowded dance area. Matt *was* a wild dancer. He threw in crazy hip-hop moves that had Haley laughing so hard she could barely keep up with him. She was having a great time.

The music changed, and the band began a song that

had a strong, pulsing rhythm. Matt did more hip-hop moves, and Haley found herself stomping and clapping along. She felt loose and relaxed.

"Watch this," Matt called. He clapped his hands and stomped in a complicated pattern.

Haley raised an eyebrow. "Oh, yeah? Watch this!" she cried back. She made up a crazy pattern of stomping and clapping on her own. Matt stared at her intently. Suddenly Haley realized the moves seemed familiar. Her mouth dropped open in surprise. She hadn't made up the moves. She was doing her new stomp-dance sequence!

"What was *that*?" Matt asked, impressed.

Haley tried the moves again. Dancing to the music made her forget her nervousness. Without Blake watching her and without Patrick frowning at her, the moves came easily. Haley wasn't even thinking about the steps. She was just feeling great, moving to the music. Before she knew it, she had completed the entire routine without a single mistake.

Matt's eyes widened in admiration. Haley laughed with pleasure. The difficult steps weren't difficult anymore. They were easy!

"That looked fantastic," Matt told her.

"I know!" she cried. "It's from my new pairs routine. And this is the first time I ever got the whole thing right!"

"Congratulations." Matt grinned. "Maybe I bring you good luck."

Haley gazed at him happily. "Definitely!"

16

Haley checked her watch for what seemed like the millionth time. Where was her father? She had been feeling great about getting the dance sequence down. But her good mood was fading. Haley gazed again through the glass doors of the Olympic arena. Still no sign of her dad's car.

"I wonder where he is," Haley said in a small voice.

"I feel like we've spent this whole vacation waiting for your dad," Tori complained. "Waiting for dinner, waiting to be picked up, waiting for him to come home."

"I'm sure he's on his way," Haley said. "Besides, we shouldn't complain. After all, he's the one who got us these tickets."

"You mean his *assistant* got them," Tori pointed out.

"So?" Haley shot back. "What's the difference? My father's busy, that's all."

"Yeah—*too* busy, if you ask me," Tori grumbled.

Haley shot her a sharp glance. What was Tori trying to say? That Haley's father didn't care about them?

Haley turned away. Tori had some nerve. Right then Haley almost wished Tori hadn't come on this trip.

The two girls waited in silence. Finally Mr. Arthur pulled up in his car and honked the horn. Haley and Tori hurried outside.

"Hi, girls. Sorry I'm late," Mr. Arthur called. He sighed. "It's not easy to fit in a family schedule with this new job. I have to be available in case any problems crop up. It's tough trying to balance everything."

He paused as Haley and Tori climbed into the car. "I have something else to tell you, Haley," he said slowly. "And I'm afraid you're not going to like it."

Haley's stomach clenched nervously. "What is it?" she asked.

"I'm going to have to cut your trip short. I need to go to Albany this weekend. You two will have to leave on Thursday," Mr. Arthur explained. "I'm sorry, girls."

"But . . . then we won't get to spend any time together, Dad!" Haley burst out.

"I'm sorry, honey. I wish you could stay longer. It's just bad timing," her father said. "I wanted to see you, and I knew how much you wanted to be here for the Worlds. I'm afraid I just didn't realize how hard it would be for me to spend time with you. I promise I'll make it up to you next trip."

Haley felt like crying. "Why can't you skip this meeting?" she shouted.

"Honey, I've gone on trips before," he told her.

Haley suddenly realized that her father was right. He *had* traveled a lot when he lived in Seneca Hills. But it had never been a big deal because Haley's mom was there to take care of things.

Haley frowned. What would she do if she were living in Canada full-time? What if her dad had to go on one of his trips then? Who would stay with her? Could she stay by herself?

She doubted that either of her parents would like that idea. And it didn't sound like much fun to her, either. Haley was quiet the rest of the way home.

Back at the apartment, her dad said a quick good night. He seemed so anxious about work that Haley softened a little.

"Thanks for getting us the tickets, Dad," she said.

"My pleasure, champ," he answered. "See you in the morning, girls."

He disappeared into his room to work again.

Haley turned to Tori. "I'm sorry we have to go back home early."

Tori shrugged. "That's okay. It's not your fault."

"Yeah." Haley plopped down on the couch. "I guess you were right, Tori. My dad hasn't been around for us much." Suddenly Haley realized that if Tori hadn't come along, she would have spent her vacation almost completely alone! "Tori," Haley said, "I'm really sorry I got mad at you before."

"Me too," said Tori. "Anyway, it *was* nice of your dad to get the tickets. Even if they were for pairs."

Haley sighed. "I really thought this trip would be different."

Tori smiled. "I had fun at the party tonight. And the Worlds were fantastic." She laughed. "But I'm definitely *not* going to eat junk food when we get back!"

Haley laughed.

"Hey, Tori," she said, "I almost forgot! Remember when Matt and I were dancing? Well, I did the whole stomp-dance sequence. The new one that Patrick and I kept messing up."

"You're kidding!" Tori exclaimed. "Even the really hard part with the claps and stuff?"

"All of it," Haley said. "And it wasn't hard at all. It was fun. Watch."

Haley leaped off the sofa. She ran through the sequence flawlessly, ending with a giant bow.

Her friend burst into applause. "That looked terrific!" Tori cried. "I can't believe you and Patrick had so much trouble with it."

Haley grinned. "Me either. I can't wait to get home and show Patrick!"

"You can't?" Tori stared at her with a strange expression on her face.

"Of course," Haley went on. "It'll look fantastic. Wait till we show you the whole routine." She paused and gazed at Tori.

Tori's mouth had dropped open in surprise.

Haley frowned. "What's wrong? Didn't you like the steps?"

"Haley, do you realize what you just said?" Tori demanded, her hands on her hips.

"What?" Haley asked in confusion.

"You said you can't wait to go home." Tori shook her head. "To Seneca Hills," she added.

"Oh!" Haley grinned sheepishly. "Oops."

She collapsed back onto the sofa bed. "I guess that *is* what I want," she admitted. "I really want to go home. To Seneca Hills."

"Yes!" Tori shouted.

Haley grew thoughtful. "I know I'll still miss my dad," she said. "But this vacation showed me something. Living with him up here just wouldn't work out. I mean, he loves me and all. But I'd be alone most of the time. I'd hate that. And the food—it's *terrible*!" She shuddered.

Tori laughed. "I'm so glad you're coming back home. I would have missed you *so* much."

"Me too," Haley replied. "If I stayed here long enough, I'd probably even miss Morgan!" She grinned. "But seriously, I don't want to give up Silver Blades. And since I can live with only one parent, it should be my mom. She knows how to run a family a lot better than my dad does."

Haley felt happier than she had in days. She and Tori climbed into bed and pulled up the comforter.

"You're doing the right thing," Tori whispered.

"I know," Haley whispered back. "I mean, it was fun to visit Canada. And Matt was a terrific partner." She paused. "But moving here won't solve my problems," she continued. "My parents would still be living apart. I would still have to get used to that."

"Well, maybe your dad could visit you next time," Tori told her. "I mean, no matter where you are, he's still your dad."

"You're right. Good night, Tori," Haley said.

Tori yawned. "Good night," she answered.

Haley snuggled under the covers. What Tori said is true, she thought. We might be living in separate places. But one thing is the same. My family is still my family.

But is Patrick still my partner?

17

Haley sailed into the end of the stomp-dance combination, clapping her hands and following with six alternating knee lifts and clap-stomp-turn combinations. She did a half turn and skidded to a stop before gliding happily over to where Patrick, Blake, and Kathy were watching her.

"Haley, you've really gotten the combination down!" Blake congratulated her.

"It looks very good," Kathy agreed.

Patrick shook his head in amazement. "You're much better at it now than I am. I can't believe you just went skating off to Canada and came back with this routine totally worked out. You were supposed to be on vacation!"

"I was!" Haley responded with a grin. "And that's just the reason I was able to get it. Like I told you, I was dancing at the Worlds party and suddenly it came out perfectly. I guess I finally started having fun with it!"

"That's the secret," Blake agreed.

"Some secret," said Patrick, rolling his eyes a little. "Okay, Haley, come on. Show me how you did that again. But a little more slowly this time."

Haley launched into the combination again, with Patrick watching her closely. After trying to follow her a few times, Patrick did the combination slightly better. She ran through it again, speeding up a bit. He kept up. They faced each other, grinning as they sped up the tempo more and more, and finally burst out laughing with pleasure. Patrick had it!

"All right!" Kathy yelled in approval. "That looks much better!"

"I guess you don't need me around anymore," said Blake. "Congratulations, guys." He gave a little wave and skated off.

Haley and Patrick continued to practice getting their timing together. By the end of their session, they had made real progress in their routine. Haley was really pleased. Doing the stomp-dance combination with Patrick was so much fun!

"That was amazing, Haley," Patrick said with a smile as they stepped off the ice. "I guess Canada was really good for you. It sounds like you had a lot of fun, too."

"I did," Haley answered, slipping on her skate guards. "It was good to see my dad. The rink was first-rate, and I met some nice skaters, too."

"I guess we're really lucky that we didn't lose you to the Canadians, then," Patrick said jokingly.

Haley had to laugh. "I guess so," she responded. "But mostly I'm glad that we're not fighting anymore," she added shyly.

"Never again," Patrick promised solemnly.

"Never again," Haley agreed. "See you tomorrow, Patrick!"

As Haley skated happily off the ice, she almost bumped into Alex, who was just ending his practice with Nikki.

"Hey, you looked good out there," Alex said with a grin. "You must have worked on that sequence a lot up in Canada."

"Yeah, I guess," Haley answered. She smiled. Alex was so cute. Even cuter than Matt, she decided.

"Well, it's nice to have you back," Alex said, his eyes meeting hers.

"Thanks," said Haley, gazing back at him. "It's nice to be back. Really nice."

"Well, um . . ." Alex hesitated for a moment. "Listen, now that you're back, maybe we can finally, you know, go out, like we talked about. Maybe next weekend or something."

"That sounds great," said Haley, feeling her face flush a little.

"Okay," Alex replied. "Well, I guess I'll see you to-morrow."

"See you tomorrow," Haley sang back happily. She

watched as Alex headed toward the boys' locker room. I'm so glad to be back in Seneca Hills, she said to herself with delight.

Haley burst into the girls' locker room, whistling. She pushed the swinging door so hard that it almost smashed into Tori.

"Hey! Watch it!" Tori yelped. "We know you're happy to be home, Haley, but you don't have to rip the door off its hinges," she joked.

"Sorry, Tori, I wasn't paying attention," Haley apologized. "I'm just in such a good mood!"

Haley stepped into the locker room and saw her other friends changing after practice. Nikki looked over the door of her locker at Haley with a grin. Amber gave her a wave.

"That was some practice you and Patrick had," Nikki commented.

"Yeah," Martina agreed. "You guys were really going. I was impressed."

"I'm so happy we finally got it together," Haley declared. "I love our new routine. It makes me feel terrific."

"I know what you mean," Amber said. "When my skating goes well, everything seems to go well."

"I wish we were still on vacation, though," Martina said. "When I woke up this morning, I was so sorry that it was a school day again."

"Me too," Haley told her. "My mom practically had to kick me out the door this morning. I stayed up so late finishing my homework. I had a ton to make up. Ugh!"

Nikki pulled her parka out of her locker. "Well, speaking of homework, I'd better go. I have to read a whole chapter for social studies and do a book report. See you guys tomorrow!"

"Bye!" Haley said. "I'd better check that Kathy is ready to go. See you guys in the morning."

"Good night, Haley," said Amber.

Haley gave her a smile as she grabbed her things from her locker. Then she headed down the hall to Kathy's office and stuck her head in the door.

"Knock, knock," Haley said. "Hi, Kathy."

"Hi, Haley," Kathy answered. She briskly shuffled together some papers on her desk. "Why don't we go now? I'll finish these schedules tomorrow."

"Great!" Haley replied.

Haley and Kathy headed out of the office and down the hall to the exit. As they were leaving the building, Haley heard a car horn. She turned around and was surprised to see her mom's car. What's she doing here? Haley wondered.

Mrs. Arthur rolled down her window and called out, "Haley! I'm going to drive you home today! Hi, Kathy!" Haley's mom waved at her coach.

Amazing! Haley thought. She *never* comes to pick me up!

"That's a nice surprise, huh?" Kathy commented. "Well, I'll see you in the morning, then."

"Okay, Kathy. Bye," Haley said. She started toward her mother's car. I wonder what's going on, she thought. What could be so important that Mom would take off early from work and come pick me up at the rink?

18

Haley raced to her mother's black Pathfinder and yanked open the car door.

"Hi, Mom! Why are you picking me up?" Haley asked. She hopped into the front seat and threw her bags in the back.

"I thought we'd surprise you," her mother answered.

We? Haley thought. She whirled around.

"Hi, Haley," Morgan greeted her from the backseat.

"You're both here?" Haley gaped at her mom.

"I had to leave the office early today to meet a client," her mother told her. "So I picked up Morgan from riding and swung by to get you, too." She glanced at her watch. "It feels strange not to be in the office at this hour."

Haley and Morgan exchanged curious looks.

Mrs. Arthur gazed across the Ice Arena parking lot.

Haley noticed that her mother didn't seem to be looking at anything in particular.

"Is something wrong, Mom?" Haley finally asked.

Mrs. Arthur shook her head. "No. Actually, I have a surprise for you girls." She took a deep breath. "When we leave here, we're going to pick your dad up at the airport."

Haley's heart skipped a beat. "Dad's coming home?"

"For how long?" Morgan asked.

"Just for a couple of days," her mother answered. "He finished his business in Albany and decided to come see us."

"Is he going to stay at the hotel again?" Haley asked. She couldn't help hoping that her father would stay at home with them. But she guessed that wasn't too likely. After all, she reminded herself, her parents were separated.

"Yes, he will, Hals," Mrs. Arthur said gently. She glanced at Haley and Morgan. "Your father and I have talked it over. We decided that he should spend as many weekends here as possible. That way he can see a little more of you girls," her mother finished.

"Wow!" Haley cried. That was good news! Haley was going to see her dad much more often than she'd expected.

"It doesn't mean we're getting back together," her mom warned. "But we both think it's important for him to keep seeing both of you."

"I'm glad," Morgan said quietly.

"Me too. It's a terrific idea, Mom," Haley added.

"I'm glad you think so," her mother replied. "But girls, I want you to decide which weekends to spend with your dad. It's your choice."

"It is?" Haley asked in surprise. She wasn't used to this. Her mother never let her be in charge of things.

"Well, these decisions affect *your* life, too," her mother replied. "Your dad is important, but you also need to leave time for friends."

"Yeah," Morgan added quietly.

"Since when do you care?" Haley asked her sister.

"Haley!" her mother scolded. "Your sister could really use your help. It isn't easy for her to get through all this."

"But she never even seems upset," Haley protested.

"That's not true!" Morgan exclaimed.

"Hals, think about it," her mother urged. "Morgan doesn't come out and say what she feels. It's hard for her to admit when something's wrong. But she's just as upset as you are."

It was true that Morgan had trouble talking about her feelings. Haley gazed at her sister, who was staring down at her lap.

"Whenever Morgan's really upset, she gets more in-volved in riding. She uses riding to escape whatever's troubling her," her mother finished.

"That's what I do!" Haley cried. "With skating, I mean. When I'm skating, I forget about stuff that's bothering me, too."

She was thoughtful a moment. "I'm sorry, Morgan," she told her sister. "Maybe we can be better friends from now on."

"Okay," Morgan said happily.

"I appreciate that, Haley," her mother added.

Haley saw that her mother had tears in her eyes. "Your support is very important to me," her mom went on. "You may not realize it, but I need you, too."

"You do?" Haley asked, astonished. "I never knew that."

Her mother seemed surprised. "But we're family. Nothing is more precious to me than you and Morgan!" Mrs. Arthur reached out and squeezed Haley's hand. "I want you to be happy with all the decisions we make. After all, this is the only family any of us have."

"I guess you're right," Haley said.

"We have to help each other through this," her mother continued.

"We will," Haley promised. "I was a little worried about Dad being so far away," she admitted. "And I'd still like it better if you and Dad got back together," she went on. "But I understand if you can't."

Mrs. Arthur squeezed her daughter's hand. "Haley, I don't say this as often as I should. But I think you're really special."

"Thanks, Mom," Haley responded. "You and Morgan are special, too."

Haley, Morgan, and their mom exchanged hugs. "Well, we'd better get to the airport. It's almost time to pick up your dad."

Her family might still be apart, but things were beginning to settle down. Haley was getting used to the idea of her parents living apart. And she realized now that she wasn't going to lose either of them.

Her mother eased the car out of the parking lot. Haley gazed out the window as they drove through the familiar streets. The lights of downtown had never seemed brighter. Her favorite store windows seemed almost like old friends as they passed. Many things had changed. But it was still great to be back in Seneca Hills.

I guess it's true, she thought. There really is no place like home.

school, has a plan that's sure to get her into *big* trouble. Could this be the end of Jill's skating career?

#5: The Perfect Pair

Nikki Simon and Alex Beekman are the perfect pair on the ice. But off the ice there's a big problem. Suddenly Alex is sending Nikki gifts and asking her out on dates. Nikki wants to be Alex's partner in pairs but not his girlfriend. Will she lose Alex when she tells him? Can Nikki's friends in Silver Blades find a way to save her friendship with Alex *and* her skating career?

#6: Skating Camp

Summer's here, and Jill can't wait to join her best friends from Silver Blades at skating camp. It's going to be just like old times. But things have changed since Jill left Silver Blades to train at a famous ice academy. Tori and Danielle are spending all their time with another skater, Haley Arthur, and Nikki has a big secret that she won't share with anyone. Has Jill lost her best friends forever?

#7: The Ice Princess

Tori's favorite skating superstar, Elyse Taylor, is in town, and she's staying with Tori! When Elyse promises to teach Tori her famous spin, Tori's sure they'll become the best of friends. But Elyse isn't the sweet champion everyone thinks she is. And she's going to make problems for Tori!

#8: Rumors at the Rink

Haley can't believe it—Kathy Bart, her favorite coach in the whole world, is quitting Silver Blades! Haley's sure it's all her fault. Why didn't she listen when everyone told her to stop playing practical jokes on Kathy? With Kathy gone, Haley knows she'll never win the next big competition. She has to make Kathy change her mind—no matter what. But will Haley's secret plan work?

#9: Spring Break

Jill is home from the Ice Academy, and everyone is treating her like a star. And she loves it! It's like a dream come true—especially when she meets cute, fifteen-year-old Ryan McKensey. He's so fun and cool—and he happens to be her number-one fan! The only problem is that he doesn't understand what it takes to be a professional athlete. Jill doesn't want to ruin her chances with such a great guy. But will dating Ryan destroy her future as an Olympic skater?

#10: Center Ice

It's gold medal time for Tori—she just knows it! The next big competition is coming up, and Tori has a winning routine. Now all she needs is that fabulous skating dress her mother promised her! But Mrs. Carsen doesn't seem to be interested in Tori's skating anymore—not since she started dating a new man in town. When Mrs. Carsen tells Tori she's not going to the competition, Tori decides enough is enough. She has a plan that will change everything—forever!

#11: A Surprise Twist

Danielle's on top of the world! All her hard work at the rink has paid off. She's good. Very good. And Dani's new English teacher, Ms. Howard, says she has a real flair for writing—she might even be the best writer in her class. Trouble is, there's a big skating competition coming up—*and* a writing contest. Dani's stumped. Her friends and family are counting on her to skate her best. But Ms. Howard is counting on her to write a winning story. How can Dani choose between skating and her new passion?

#12: The Winning Spirit

A group of Special Olympics skaters is on the way to Seneca Hills! The skaters are going to pair up with the Silver Blades members in a mini-competition. Everyone in Silver Blades thinks Nikki Simon is really lucky—her Special Olympics partner is Carrie, a girl with Down syndrome who's one of the best visiting skaters. But Nikki can't seem to warm up to the idea of skating with Carrie. In fact, she seems to be hiding something . . . but what?

#13: The Big Audition

Holiday excitement is in the air! Jill Wong, one of Silver Blades' best skaters, is certain she will win the leading role of Clara in the *Nutcracker on Ice* spectacular. Until young skater Amber Armstrong comes along. At first Jill can't believe that Amber is serious competition. But she had better believe it—and fast! Because she's about to find herself completely out of the spotlight.

#14: Nutcracker on Ice

Nothing is going Jill Wong's way. She hates her role in the *Nutcracker on Ice* spectacular. And she's hardly on the ice long enough to be noticed! To top it all off, the Ice Academy coaches seem awfully impressed with Jill's main rival, Amber Armstrong. Jill has worked so hard to return to the Academy, and now she might lose her chance. Does Jill have what it takes to save her lifelong dream?

Super Edition #1: Rinkside Romance

Tori, Haley, Nikki, and Amber are at the Junior Nationals, where a figure skater's dreams can really come true! But Amber's trying too hard, and her skating is awful. Tori's in trouble with an important judge. Nikki and Alex are fighting so much they might not make it into the competition. And someone is sending them all mysterious love notes! Are their skating dreams about to turn into nightmares?

Do you have a younger brother or sister? Maybe he or she would like to meet Jill Wong's little sister Randi and her friends in the exciting new series SILVER BLADES FIGURE EIGHTS. Look for these titles at your bookstore or library:

ICE DREAMS
STAR FOR A DAY

and coming soon:

THE BEST ICE SHOW EVER!
BOSSY ANNA